COUPLER
by Susan S. Sledge

Published by Conduit Publishing
8210 Paluxy Hwy,
Tolar, TX 76476
email: susan.sledge@sledgedistillery.com

Book and cover design: Michael Campbell, MC Writing Services
Cover photo: Teppakorn Tongboonto, iStockPhoto

ISBN: 978-1-62660-166-6

Coupler

by

SUSAN S. SLEDGE

This book is dedicated to
Chaynee Cooper (1997-2001),
Gage Cooper (1998-2003),
Tyler Riale (1985-2011),
Briggs Berry (1996-2014)
and their loving parents
who I admire beyond words.

CONTENTS

PROLOGUE:
A JOURNEY SHARED

WELCOME TO THIS INCREDIBLE STORY that links you and me. No matter what year you were born, country, gender, political persuasion, DNA make-up, wealth, or any other label you may be wearing, we were individually, uniquely hand-crafted, and placed into one point in time for a particular purpose on a massive journey. During our time here, we will share in the same narrative and stand as co-authors, possibly without knowing we are taking part in a grand story.

This story is a fictional answer to many thoughtful moments after visiting friends with children in the hospital. Sadly, their medical struggles overtook their children's lives and, in some cases, their marriages. It seemed so unfair to return home to my healthy family while theirs were struggling to make it through the day. As they asked me "why" this was happening, I asked God the same thing. Over decades, God gave me this story to help organize the concepts of time and eternity, life and death, and the knowledge that what seems real here is not the full picture of reality.

You might not buy into the whole "Perfectly and wonderfully made for a great purpose" kind of thing, and honestly, I don't blame you. It takes some fortitude to have faith in "all things working out for good" when facing tough times. Inevitably the question arises, "If we were all created in God's image for a purpose, then why do heart-breaking things happen during this lifetime?" I have asked myself and God this question so often that it has led me to believe it can't be answered with our present, seen circumstances. There must be more. Still, the truth can stand even if our present circumstances don't seem to support it. There will come the fullness of time where all will become clear. Until then, we are trusting our Maker and each other the best we can to manage life's mysteries.

I hope that sharing this story with you will provide insight and clarity to your human experience as it has done to mine. I suggest you let the story unfold and awaken your divine imagination of what is or could be happening at this moment in time.

CHAPTER 1

The massive, arched canopy with white, tree-like columns spanning an undefinable space allow for Victorian age trains to rest before a long journey. Light-filled skies provide the perfect backdrop for a mesmerizing, translucent ceiling that casts light into the entire station. Each train car is antique at first glance, but upon examination, they are strangely inclusive of design elements, finishes, and colors from almost every age. Intricately painted stones, each a piece of art, invite you into their story. The stones provide an exquisite base for the tracks made of perfectly polished gold. The tracks quiver at the anticipation of launching its cargo and passengers on a journey. The golden tracks sing a timeless song of existence so lovely and primal it is intoxicating. Each car is completely unique in color and shape and curiosity is awaken. You want to look at them all at one time but can't because the details in each one is overwhelmingly beautiful to the point you feel as if your eyes could never fully communicate to your brain what you are seeing. Your mind searches stored memories and cataloged facts of what you are seeing but you come up empty. You have no frame of reference for the magnitude of this place and these amazing trains. Your spirit is stirred up, looking for meaning and desperately trying to understand why these trains exist, their purpose, and how you fit into all of this.

As you step towards one train car, you notice a number proudly displayed as a banner across the car. It catches your eye because the numeric banner is the one unifying factor among all the cars. Every car is completely unique in design, and you wonder how such a variety could be possible. They are sequentially numbered, and instinctively you know that this train's purpose is tied to those numbers. As this *revelation sinks in, you feel truth permeate your body like warm butter pouring out on you from your head to toe. It feels like an awakening rather than learning something new. How could you have forgotten something so significant? What do these numbers mean?*

Between the cars, couplers exist to connect the two with its massive iron construction perfectly made to adjoin car to car with an eternal bond so that the combination of cars could never change and ensure no interruptions in the journey. The coupler is triple secured by a massive chain whose colorful links are semi-transparent and, like the tracks, vibrate with the same timeless song. The coupler and chain become one huge mechanism that undergirds the railcar, and its colorful reflection gently emerges from beneath the cars, illuminating the tracks.

Your amazement is interrupted by the sweet sound of laughter whose voices wash over you like a familiar, warm, cozy, love-filled quilt draped over your shoulders and embracing your innermost being. Hearing their voices is laced with a deep-seated knowing that you are about to peek into the beginning, the very moment of your inception. Your story begins here not exclusively as something unique to only you but as a collective moment unique to every one of us.

You glance to your right, and there they sit at a beautifully carved table in the middle of this massive station interacting as they have always done, fully devoted, wildly entertaining, inspiring, and purposeful. Oh, how wonderful is the life-giving breath in which you take Him in. It is addicting, easy like ingesting a child's giggle, but all-encompassing and rattles every cell of your body. They are everything that ever mattered or will ever matter, and you smile knowing that their presence is not only fitting but provides absolute confidence in knowing that everything is as it should be. Your mind relaxes knowing that it is no longer burdened with defining the moment with meaning because being in their presence is the meaning.

Abba is a handsome, distinguished, older man with a rugged face, deserving the comfort and sensibility of overalls and boots. His glance is one of approval and shoots into your veins, fortifying your soul with all His experience and confidence painstakingly acquired yet simply gifted to you with only a glance. As He laughs, the atmosphere reverberates with soft undertones of thunder that thump in your chest, causing goosebumps on the top of your head.

Jesus, a man who looks to be about thirty-five years old with handsome, rugged features and expressive eyes, is dressed simply in blue jeans and a well-worn concert t-shirt. You recognize the band because it's your personal favorite and you saw them on the same tour with college friends. It was a night you would never forget. At first, you think it is a coincidence but then you have come to believe that there are no coincidences. Jesus wearing it today is a signal from Him that you are supposed to be here, and He shares the same likes, even in rock bands. His smile draws you in from deep within your guts and pulls you outward directly into His mesmerizing eyes. The wrinkles in each corner squinch together to frame His face to direct every thought and emotion so that you can behold and embrace Him, soul to soul. You cannot help but smile because you have shared so much with Him that His laughter perfectly activates your joy into a fountain of laughter, and likewise, His sorrow burdens your heart.

Their conversation is fueled by the Holy Spirit, a young man in the form of a hologram. Although in form, He is similar to Abba and Jesus, He is more fluid, brilliantly colorful, and exists in a totally different manner than them. He has Jesus' eyes that draw you in and Abba's confidence but has a presence that swirls around like the playful yet powerful wind. Holy Spirit is the connection between the three of them, and He embodies the tribunal power birthed from their existence to weave together souls into a shared experience, a beautiful tapestry of love.

Jesus becomes excited as you notice an exquisite, elaborately decorated book that sits among them. The leather binding encases ivory pages with gilded edges. It is a work of art with great significance. Even the table they have gathered around has the express purpose of displaying the book. It is a ledger, and instinctively you understand it is a record of something the men were discussing. Although you don't understand the specifics, you are sure it pertains to you as well as everyone else who has ever existed. At that very second, you wonder about its meaning. Holy Spirit provides you instant knowledge (it's His specialty) that you are witnessing a discussion proceeding the creation of the heavens, earth, and man.

You are allowed access to their conversation and learn they are talking about their most important creation, Adam and Eve. Although man will be created as a perfect representation of Abba, Jesus, and Holy Spirit collectively, they also know that man will struggle to accept them or anything beyond what they can see, feel, touch, or reason within their immediate surroundings. You watch them interact as they set about remedying this dilemma.

With a semi-serious expression, Abba says to the others, "They won't understand unless we give them a beginning and an end."

Jesus replies, "Let's create clues their brains and bodies can easily embrace." They determine that man needs a way to mark and judge interactions with each other as well as all that transpires between heaven and earth. Without set points of revelation, man's brain will not be able to organize the story enough to feed the spirit and soul. He will crave knowledge of the past, present, and future to assess his existence and purpose rightly. Abba suggests they create "time," a temporary state on earth marked by light in the day and dark in the night. It will rotate from day to night regularly, and man will be able to mark it and provide meaning through it.

Holy Spirit wholeheartedly, and like everything else He does, shows absolute enthusiasm for the creative process. He comments, "Let's integrate messages, signs, and wonders between our world and theirs, so they know us and know they aren't alone."

Jesus excitedly adds, "We need them to know how much we love them and that their lives really matter. They influence us and everyone else who came before them, those with them, and even those coming after them."

Holy Spirit responds, "Totally, I agree. Time it is. Our gift."

They all nod in agreement and Jesus says, "So, we agree. We're going to do this," and when He says it, there seems to be another meaning, a flicker of acknowledgment among their faces that you don't quite understand but sense it adds weight and impact to the moment.

Abba, with a huge smile spreading across His face, says, "All aboard…" They laugh, and the sound fills your soul as you watch them high-five and celebrate.

The purpose of this amazing train station with uniquely designed trains becomes instantly clear. Every train car is a moment in time consisting of seconds, minutes, hours, and days, connecting together into weeks, months, and years. Every person is created to align with time and instinctively organize their lives within its rhythm. These beautiful trains will encapsulate time while proceeding through eternity. The timeless ones are able to access earthly time within a train car and are free to move from car to car at will. The numbers so beautifully noted on the outside mark a specific year and are moving through eternity in sequential order. All cars, times, and epics are connected by the coupler and chain system inspired by Holy Spirit's handiwork.

As you look around this magnificent train station and realize that you have just witnessed the creation of time, you stand amazed. You suddenly learn another facet of these three now revealed, adding to your ever-expanding perspective of the Creators.

Suddenly, all the light within your vision begins to contract, and you feel as if you are being sucked out of reality. The trains begin to move at a high rate of speed, dashing here, there, and everywhere. You are amazed at how alive the cars are; the colors, the speed, and the ease in which they glide through the dark expanse remind you of a massive row of houses with open doors and windows emitting an enthralling light inviting you to come and hear their story. Beams of light dance in, through, under, over, and around the trains as if dancing in delight that the long-awaited journey has now begun. You are fully aware that being in the Creators' presence is an honor, and for every question answered, it prompts hundreds more in its place.

Once again, you are distracted by the choreographed network of trains and witnessing their free-flowing journey from a viewpoint far above when one train car captivates your attention. It's as if the whole train slows down in only one section to make sure you notice the car is marked with DM-1967-0012-0303. The car's oblong shape is distinctive, with its rough weathered exterior made of hand-hewed cedar planks. The ceiling is made of stained glass in the most brilliant colors ever imagined. The contrast between the lumber and glass makes you wonder if you like it or not, but then you notice that within the massive ceiling design, there is a small symbol that has an intoxicating effect. The symbol represents an infinity sign, but the loops are also butterfly wings. It draws you in so much so that you are instantly transported to the rooftop and find yourself on a mysterious quest to learn about its contents.

As you peek into the roof, light from within illuminates into a warm shade of pure love. It envelops into a warm, familiar embrace, but not familiar in the sense that you know it, but rather lived it in your own time, your own place, your own car. The light moves through you, and you rest into it, not wanting anything to ever change but to stay in this moment, moving through time. Your cells come into agreement with the light, and your questions haven't been answered but rather multiply at a rapid pace, but you rest into it not really caring because you know the questions are creating a foundation that girds you and provides security for the answers that are sure to come.

The light swirls around you, and you instinctively know you are invited inside this special car. You immediately feel honored knowing its contents are wisdom itself, opening the deepest of truth to you. You view two young girls, each with golden brown hair, sleeping in their snug twin beds that fill a quiet room. As you get closer to the train car, the light ushers you through and into where your surroundings are miraculously transformed from the eternal realm to joining the two *little girls in a dramatically different place. It feels so different from what you remember. You confidently carry a peace with you that was elusive when you were there. It is a sacred moment, and you accept the invitation to become one with this particular point in time, knowing that you will be forever changed, fulfilling a yearning you have had from inception.*

CHAPTER 2

As the light moves deeper down the long train of cars, it pulls you away from the little girls and into another car with a gentle flow that you melt into. Although the new scene is unexpectedly gruesome, you have peace and feel oddly untouched by the pain you are witnessing. A man is pinned between two earthly railcars that, in contrast, seem so dark and dirty compared to the ones from the heavenly train station. A woman and a little girl are sobbing through their tears, "Daddy, please. Daddy. I'm not strong. Not like you. I need you, Daddy. Daddy, don't go!" Bystanders look bewildered and helpless. Some look away trying to erase the situation, but they cannot cut off the sound of sorrow still engaging their hearts.

As the man struggles to breathe, the eternal light that is his companion goes into his body and expands around him, pulsing with every breath. You suddenly notice Abba has been standing alongside him, and Jesus has the man's head and shoulders in His arms. Jesus whispers into the man's ear while Abba puts His hand out. The man's soul, which you can now distinguish from his body, nods, raises up to a standing position, and takes a step towards Abba. He and Abba embrace and exchange a few words, and the man nods in agreement.

The man turns to the bystanders and notices a woman standing behind the screaming little girl, not knowing how to help. He walks over to her and whispers in her ear, "I'm leaving now. She needs your help to be strong. I trust you with her." The woman takes a deep breath, leans over, and touches the little girl's shoulder. He puts his hand on hers as she comforts his daughter, and then he strokes his little girl's golden brown hair as he did almost every night before putting her to *bed. Jesus puts His arm around the man. The man looks at Him with a calm expression full of love and acceptance for all that is happening. As the man turns back towards Abba, Jesus's attention shifts to the little girl who He embraces. Light illuminates the moment.*

Just as gently as you arrived into this scene, you feel the motion of being pulled back away from the scene and are fully aware that time is shifting again; You are moving fast down a long line of cars. Your curiosity is peaked, but it isn't something you must discover, but rather something that is being revealed. It is such an odd thing, even now having been here so long, to experience surprises and mysteries with the absence of fear. There was once a time when fear was the precipice in any surprise or mystery.

You hear a voice as you travel. It is the little girl's voice that just witnessed her father's death. She is speaking to you. You don't look for her because you know she isn't there in physical form. She says, "That was the day I was left utterly alone. Well, maybe not totally alone. I became personally acquainted with death, my new companion." How was she narrating her own story and with such maturity and wisdom perched on every word? So much is happening at one time. You are moving through time from car to car making quick stops, hearing voices, and before you can process the little girl's message, an image appears in your mind's eye.

Your mind sees a picture of an old woman sitting on a park bench. Next to her is a walker with a bag of groceries hanging on to the handle. Her salt and pepper hair is raised into a bun with little pieces framing her face. Time has worn her features into deep crevasses of worry and disappointment. Her intoxicating cornflower blue eyes are tired but, as promised, she continues to make an effort to get out of bed every morning and live another day.

The woman is teleconferencing with a middle-aged man who resembles a modern version of Jesus. The conversation is already in process, and you hear the woman say, "Oh, yes, he's real. Don't let anyone tell you otherwise. I've known him almost all my life. Actually, he stole my life as I knew it and gave me this lonely existence. My heart still beats, but I can assure you, I've been dead for a very long time."

The man responds, "Can you remember when you felt alive?"

She chuckles slightly, then shuts her eyes in a moment of pain, "Oh, that's easy. Every day until my twelfth birthday. It was a time that I knew my life really mattered. I feel stupid for believing it now but my father learned it from his father and I guess they didn't know any better."

You are wondering who this woman is and why she is talking with Jesus. So many questions bouncing around in your head. Does she know she is talking to Jesus? Is she on one of these trains, and if so, which one? Who were they talking about knowing? It seemed so strange but significant.

Your thoughts and vision of the old lady begin to fade away as your attention is directed back toward your destination, car #DM-1967-0012-0700. It is the same stained glass, cedar planked train that invited your attention after leaving the station. As you enter into the train car, you view a small clapboard house alone in a pasture next to a dusty train track. Your focus is directed towards the early morning sunlight directing itself through a second-story window. You travel with the light into the room and a feeling of great love washes over you. It is the same quiet room you saw when you originally entered the train.

The old woman is no longer your focus but filed away for a later date. You know there are no coincidences in thoughts and experiences and appreciate the grand design of such things. The need to have answers isn't a desire any longer because in this place, you are satisfied knowing answers arrive when needed.

CHAPTER 3

Delaney is snuggled up to the far side of the bed with her nose and chin tucked peacefully under the crisp edge of the pastel sheet. She feels a cool breeze on her backside and gently smiles as her little sister, Kinsley, climbs in behind her. It is a familiar morning ritual, and their breathing becomes synchronized. The cadence of their bond is silent yet musical. After realizing the sun is about to rise, Delaney remembers this is a very special day, her twelfth birthday! She opens her eyes and rolls over, causing the ripple effect with Kinsley, and then they both witness the softness of daylight dancing across the room. The girls talk without saying a word through a hug then Kinsley plays with a piece of Delaney's hair as they smell whiffs of mother cooking breakfast downstairs. Before they utter a word to one another, the sound of a distant train causes them to jump upright out of bed like a bolt of lightning. Giggling excitedly, they scurry around the room, grabbing their shoes and coats to hurriedly run downstairs.

Their mother, Claire, is standing at the stovetop and smiles brightly as she hears the pitter patter of footsteps above her. The table is set for pancakes with brightly colored hats at each place setting. Dennis, Delaney's father, rounds the corner with a huge smile and giant bear hug to greet his girls with enthusiasm and excitement. He is also on the same mission, frantically putting on his coat, slips into his boots, and they all run out the door. Claire smiles as she watches her crazy crew ramble outside.

The happy trio race down the porch steps and sprint to the train tracks which run alongside their West Texas home. The train is barely in sight, but they know it is coming, and the anticipation is building. It is apparent that this special day belongs to Delaney as Dennis lovingly crouches down beside her and sweetly hugs her tight. Kinsley holds her sister's hand and places her small arm on her father's shoulder.

These tracks are old and tired and have been here for generations to see this young country grow. They have moved people and supplies for every imaginable occasion, and this town was established for the express purpose of building more tracks. It is now a sleepy town with little industry, but the people take great pride in working for the railway's switch center and maintenance hub. Dennis has raised his family in this home built by his grandfather. He often wonders if his grandfather meant for them to settle such deep roots in this transient town, but he never felt a desire to leave. It is home, and the dirt that blows through this town covers his skin and provides meaning to his life. It is why he is alive, and he can't imagine any place on earth more magical than this forgotten little spot on the map. He is a man of tradition, and today, he will see to it that his daughter gets the full "Kinkaid Family Experience."

As his father had done with him and his grandfather before that, they wait by the tracks as the engine approaches. Kinsley says excitedly, "Here it comes, Daddy!" and runs off towards the train. Delaney and Dennis are inspired to run after Kinsley. After some time, they find a good place to start their birthday morning ritual.

Dennis said to Delaney, "It's hard to believe my little girl is turning twelve years old today. You know…the world needed you to arrive on April 13, 1967, at—"

Delaney interrupts, "3:03 in the morning… yes, I know, Dad!" Delaney hugs her dad. Kinsley is playing around them, entertaining herself.

Dennis doesn't want Delaney to miss the meaning of this exercise. He looks into her eyes and, holding her chin, forcing her to look at him, he says, "It's super important that you know. Everyone has an arrival time, and you were—" In unison, Delaney chimes in, "Right on time."

Delaney and Dennis laugh, then he looks at her again with more "life lessons" to be taught and says, "In all of history, God wanted you to be here, at this time, and with your Momma and me."

Kinsley is playing nearby and adds, "…and me too!"

Dennis continues, "Just like this train has a specific purpose, so do you. You are carrying something to this world. Your life matters, Delaney. Don't ever forget that. No matter where your life leads, you matter." Dennis glances over at Kinsley and adds, "We all do." As she glances over at Kinsley, she sees her little sister has a lizard by its tail and is dangling it upside down.

Delaney responds, "It certainly matters to that lizard!" They are interrupted by another horn. The train is getting near.

With all the enthusiasm the girls can muster, they wave to the conductor and cheer him on to victory; then, they start counting the cars excitedly awaiting the star of the morning, the twelfth car.

One, two, three, Kinsley starts jumping around wildly in anticipation.

Four, five, six, seven, Delaney can barely contain herself. She looks further down to try and count ahead, but the gentle curve of the track keeps the remaining cars just out of sight.

Eight, nine, ten, Delaney looks at her dad, and their eyes lock on contact. It is almost here, and she wonders who is more excited, her or her dad. They always anticipate what the car will look like, the color, the type, the size, and most of all, what it is carrying. She can't wait to take a mental snapshot to take home to her mother. She will draw a picture of it and recount every minute. She will add it to the collection she has hidden under her bed in the "special box" her mother gave her as a child. It contained pressed flowers, pictures, her pet rock, a note from her first crush, and a locket she received for Christmas one year.

Eleven, what a beauty! It was a brand-new box car in brilliant green paint. It looked just like one her father had been working to repair in the rail yard. She imagined it to be a doorway to a secret forest.

Finally, she catches a glimpse of her twelfth birthday car. It was a tiny bit taller than the other cars and is painted in a dark red, rust-colored paint. She has always liked cars with character, she thought. She could only imagine all the places it had been. Oh, how she wanted to jump on one of those cars and travel to the ends of the earth. But for now, she was completely satisfied being here with her family celebrating her twelfth birthday, secure in her happy place.

Her father stands tall and looks at Delaney to see what she sees. There was a reflection of confusion on her ruffled brow that caused him to look back to the train. He sees the words "Stolen Lives" in huge, graphic graffiti consuming the entire face of the boxcar. It is artistically painted in big bubble letters of black, white, and grey.

Kinsley's response was impulsive but intuitive as she said, "Gross! Your car is so ugly!" The truth in its simplicity was jarring, and Dennis tried not to react but celebrate that it was the twelfth car. His mind was in two places at once. "Dennis mode" was wondering about the meaning of the words and confused as to the deep, fearful emotions it evoked in him. "Dad mode" was trying to recover for his sweet girl and acting like it was the greatest train car ever made.

Delaney wasn't buying it. She had always looked to her father for answers to every question. She was confident that her father held all the answers and could make sense of her feelings. It was hard for her to tell if she was disappointed, confused, scared, or mistaken because so much was coming at her. She wondered if they had counted wrong and wanted to run on the wind to get ahead of the train to try it again. She felt like her birthday had been vandalized like the graffiti-marred car. Sure, she had seen graffiti before, but "Stolen Lives" just stuck with her, somewhere deep down.

Three cars back, there was an old tanker with a tar-like material that looked like a strange, hard outer shell, followed by another tanker with tar covering it from front to back. It is obvious there was a leak, and both cars were damaged. Delaney is really shaken by the scary-looking cars, and Dennis notices as well and tries to divert her attention, "Hey, look! Your favorite color." He points to a pretty, new, green tank car. Delaney isn't so easily distracted.

As they walked back to the house, Kinsley could sense something was wrong and slid her little hand up into Delaney's. She looked up at her big sister and smiled, knowing this slight jester would be all it would take to reset the moment. Delaney politely smiled back. They walked along the tracks trying to balance carefully on the strong iron planks.

Dennis is eerily shaken by the graffiti message and is deep in thought for a few moments when he realizes he needs to bring the girls back into the moment and celebrate Delaney's big day. Dennis says to the girls, "Did you know that every train car is important and has a different purpose?"

Delaney playfully rolls her eyes. She has heard this a million times too. Kinsley is excited because she is about to nail the question her father is asking. Before they can answer, he begins by talking about the amazing engine that can pull such a train along and points out the coupler that connects each one. He reminds Delaney that each of the twelve cars is unique and wonderful because each has a specific purpose. Someone somewhere needs that particular train to arrive; each car really matters. Like her life, each year connects to the next by the strong, secure coupler, and with each year building upon the next, her unique story will greatly impact this world.

This is Kinsley's moment to chime in. "Do you remember the time you taught me to swim and blow bubbles like a fish? I think that is what Dad is talking about." Delaney chuckled because she remembered those huge cheeks full of air that would excitedly release into the water.

Dennis added his thoughts, "I remember the very first car where you came into this world kicking and screaming but the most beautiful thing I had ever seen. My heart was made new that day."

Kinsley responds with, "I wish I had twelve whole cars to call my own."

Delaney replies, "You will soon enough."

Then Kinsley looks at her father and asks in a playful tone, "Do you think they make trains long enough for someone as old as you?" They all laugh and walk back up to the porch and into the house, where Mom has breakfast ready.

Before she goes through the doorway, Delaney looks back to the train track, and her dad asks, "Penny, for your thoughts?"

Delaney can't get the cursed train out of her mind and wonders if it is a sign of something bad coming. She asks, "What does 'Stolen Lives' mean, and what was that gross stuff all over those tankers?"

Dennis responds, "It doesn't mean anything. It's just something that someone somewhere wrote in anger or desperation, but that has nothing to do with you."

Delaney considers what he is saying and looks into his eyes as a truth test. She says, "Are you sure? You say that everything matters and to watch the world for clues in solving the world's mysteries. Was that a clue? What was the meaning?" For the first time, Dennis wished his girl wasn't so smart. She is like a little life recorder well beyond her young age of twelve. Watching and storing every moment and soaking up every ounce of meaning for later use.

Claire steps out onto the porch and notices the tense moment. She looks at Dennis with a questioning look wondering why they aren't bubbling over with enthusiasm. Claire is certain something has happened but resists the urge to ask out loud. Dennis shrugs his shoulders in a preemptive response because he doesn't know what to do. Claire instinctively knows that her birthday girl needs a hug. Delaney's thoughts are interrupted by her mother's sweet hug and the announcement that the table is set and ready. Delaney snaps back into the moment and is ready for her birthday breakfast celebration. She excitedly puts on her cone-shaped hat and appreciates Claire's extra efforts to arrange chocolate chips as a smiley face on her pancakes. As they sing the birthday song, Delaney inhales it into her memory and tags it as the "best day ever."

CHAPTER 4

Getting to school was a journey and Delaney liked it that way. She had an adventurous heart and turned everything into a game. On the way, she takes her usual detour through the railyard where she tippy toes over heavily worn tracks with smooth edges due to years of service. It seemed as if every track in the world led to their small, stark, Texas town. She was so proud of this place because it was the centerpiece of the whole community. In her eyes, her daddy was the superhero of the yard. Everyone knew him, and she was told almost every day how wonderful he was, how smart, how funny, and the accolades went on and on. She never missed a chance to walk through the enormous metal gate on her way to school, way home, or both. It was as much her place as her dad's. Some people might not understand her obsession with the railyard, but it all made sense to her when she was here. She had a place here among these cars and those working there.

In the middle of the yard, Delaney takes a shortcut up a loading ramp and steps onto an open rail car. Without hesitating, she leaps out the other side onto the dry ground. The next car on a neighboring track was brightly colored with fresh red paint. In her active imagination, the rail car transformed into a traveling circus big top. She can't resist the urge to crawl inside and immediately sees proof of its existence. Taking a nearby milk crate and discarded tree branch, she pretends to be a lion tamer commanding the king of the jungle to perform for the crowd. Delaney giggles at herself as her imagination provides a world full of excitement far better than school.

Mr. Joe, a railyard worker, walks past the car and slows down to appreciate all that the circus provides. Delaney catches his glance and exchanges a bright, happy smile that they have all come to relish. Her fantasy vanishes as she remembers that she is on her way to school. She grabs her backpack and quickly scurries out the door and out of Mr. Joe's sight. Sweetly, he shakes his head and wipes his brow with the dirty rag he keeps in his back pocket. Delaney had no idea how much Mr. Joe enjoyed watching her play. It reminded him of his carefree little girl who was now grown up and all-to responsible with her own family.

As Delany rounds the end of a long chain of rail cars, she is confronted with a horrifying vision. It stops her in her tracks and her feet are locked into one place as if being in quicksand. There it is, towering menacingly above her. "Stolen Lives" is plastered in front of her like a billboard to her soul. She lets her eyes take it in from one side to the other, mapping it to her memory. She hears a restrained, eerie groan and knows only to run. Delaney is unsure if she heard the sound outload or in her mind, but regardless, she runs as fast as she can away from that thing. With each step, she is less and less scared. Her school is in sight and for the first time in her young life, she can't wait to get inside.

Being late to class isn't an oddity. Mrs. Hughes is accustomed to Delaney's last-minute, chatter-filled entry into her classroom. She loved this girl's spunk, always full of life and completely immersed in whatever is going on. Delaney has many friends, and sometimes Mrs. Hughes likes to just sit and watch her talk. Her hands fly around, her laughter is contagious, and she always attracts a crowd of people. If a new kid comes to town, Delaney is always assigned to be their buddy, giving the new student a fair chance to break into the crowd. Even though Delaney acts as if she doesn't have time for school, it is apparent she is brilliant, and her teachers wonder what she will be when she grows up. Her imagination is something to be admired, even if it doesn't fit with traditional learning models. Mrs. Hughes was delighted to have Delaney in her class and felt a special connection to her zest for life.

Delaney works hard throughout the day and checks all of Mrs. Hughes' to-do boxes in an effort to be done and free to go home! As the final bell rings, Delaney announces an enthusiastic "goodbye" to her friends and races out the door as she does every day.

A student worker with a note from the office, exhaustedly enters the room and says, "Mrs. Hughes, I have a note for Delaney Kinkaid. It's urgent!"

Mrs. Hughes, with a confused expression, responds, "You just missed her. She is the first one out of here when the bell rings." She chuckles to herself.

The student worker adds, "I don't know what this is about, but it's a pretty big deal. There were police here and everything. Mr. Crossland needs to see her *now*." Mrs. Hughes uses her own discretion and quickly reads the note. With a pale face and feeling of panic, Mrs. Hughes decides to run after Delaney to catch her. The crowded sea of students in the hallway seemed to multiply with each passing second. She was determined to find Delaney and kept weaving her way through the crowd, as a salmon trying to swim upstream.

No one beats Delaney out of the schoolyard when the bell rings. Every day, she watches the clock and hears the magnified "tick-tock, tick-tock" as she gathers up her books and prepares to set sail. This day was no different. She knew where she was headed, straight to her father's workplace because he promised to get off early to go fishing on the creek. She runs down the school's front steps and thinks she faintly hears her name be called but ignores it because it can't be more important than what she has planned next.

As she rounds the corner and the rail yard is in sight, she suddenly stops. It is a sight she cannot comprehend, and not only does her brain struggle to make sense of it, but it is also as if her body is unplugged and just stands there waiting for a download. She sees so much activity at the rail yard's entrance. People, sirens, and ambulances were coming and going, racing up and down the street. Families are gathered, and she can't help but wonder if they know something she doesn't. She usually goes through the main gate, but because of all the activity, she decides to go through a forgotten hole in the fence, making it much easier to get around. Delaney walks past two men and she notices they have strange, ghostly expressions on their faces. They are walking, not saying a word, and their faces are emotionless. She looks to her left and sees a large crowd gathered with several emergency vehicles. It was a beehive of activity and she instinctively knows the answer to her question is over there.

As she creeps up on the crowd, Mr. Joe sees her and promptly wraps her up in his arms. As he embraces her in a bear hug, he pleads, "You don't need to be here, Delaney. This isn't for you to see. You don't want to see it. You don't want to see." She couldn't see anything because her face was planted in his chest. She loved this man and trusted him, but couldn't understand why he was holding her so tight. Her natural reaction was to push away and try to break loose. His arms wrapped around her completely and she began to wonder if it was pointless to try.

Totally confused, she hears a scream in the distance, and her mind and body are alerted to the fact that it is her father's voice. The information traveled up from her feet to her head in an instant like a bolt of lightning. With an explosion of strength, she broke away from Joe's grasp and through a small peephole between the onlookers, she saw her father pinned between two trains. Even worse, he is pinched between the couplers, and the switching mechanism has his torso bound in the massive strength of its steel. Dennis is in agony and his guttural moans only add to panic that controlled the crowd. Delaney can see their collective fear and horror like an ugly cloud of smoke hanging just above the ground.

Delaney is laser-focused on Mr. Cathaway, the most important man in the yard. Several people obey Mr. Joe's instructions to hold her back as she struggles to fight her way to her father. In the grasps of strangers, Delaney locks eyes with Mr. Cathaway, who has an expression of sadness she had never seen a person wear before. She looks back at her trapped father as he opens his eyes only to recognize his precious daughter is seeing him like this. His eyes are wearing the same cloak of sadness, and she detects a note of shame in his expression.

Mr. Cathaway walks toward Delaney and squats down so that he is in her line of sight. He looks directly into her eyes, takes his hands, and gently cups her face. Delaney stops fighting and her caregivers relax their grips. She knows this man is in charge and looks straight back into his eyes. He begins to speak, and all she can think about is how sweet his voice sounds to her ears. She can barely make out the words as she wants to break loose and run to her father, but his attention is coated with a soothing presence.

The words "What's happening?" are rolling around in her head over and over. She hears Mr. Cathaway say, "Delaney, your father has been in an accident. He is stuck between the trains. When we pull the train forward, there is a chance his lungs will collapse, and he will die. Do you understand?" She then hears him ask, "Is your mother here?"

She knows enough to answer "No sir" to the question.

He looks around as if wanting to get guidance from the crowd. He focuses back on her. "Delaney, we are moving the train forward now. Do you understand what is happening? Will you let me hide your face?" Delaney felt another bolt of panic and broke loose from Mr. Cathaway. She ran with full force to her father's distorted body and fell at his feet. Reluctantly, two men scooped up the exhausted, frantic little girl and repositioned her with the crowd. Delaney didn't have the strength to fight back against their adult strength.

She heard the command to move the train forward and Delaney held her breath without looking up from the ground. As the squeaky wheels started to turn, the tightening of steel started a chain reaction that would reverberate back to the scene of the accident. As one train car moved forward, the other was locked into place releasing the ever-strong coupler from its connection.

Her father's frail, tired body slowly dropped to the ground. His silence scared her as he struggled to take a breath. Without thinking, Delaney began breathing deeper and more deliberately, hoping it would miraculously transfer to him. She waited with anticipation, but Dennis didn't expel any air or make a sound. His eyes were shut and he looked as if he were sleeping. That was it. Without any fanfare, he was gone. Mr. Cathaway's head dropped low, and he began to cry. She didn't know what scared her more. Her father's lifeless body on the ground or all the men she loved and admired looked grim, with pools of tears making patterns on their stained shirts. In an effort to be the last one to fight for him, she wiggled out of the adult's grip. They were relieved to not be the enforcers of such unintended cruelty.

Delaney covered Dennis' body with hers, kissing him and begging him to wake up. Her mind couldn't make sense of it; then, she heard a sound so horrifying that it inconceivably caused her to forget her father and look for the next tragedy. It was her mother making her way to where she and her father had crumbled. Claire was hysterical and seeing her like this was more disturbing to Delaney than seeing her father's lifeless body. It scared Delaney to her core, and as she felt this rush of fear, every other sense was heightened. Her vision was crisply focused on her mother and father but blurry everywhere else. She smelled an ugly death cloud creeping up on them like an insidious fog. Her ears could only hear the deafening sound of her mother sobbing, screaming, and wailing. Her body was numb to the touch of strangers.

Claire, usually a dignified woman, publicly begged God to bring Dennis back. Her commotion seemed like a good idea that Delaney hadn't thought to try. She joined the chorus and begged God with all her might. Periodically, Delaney would pause to see if their pleas had been heard but nothing changed.

After what seemed to be an eternity, Delaney felt strong, caring hands on her shoulders. Their impactful squeeze felt reassuring and when she felt them pull upward, it was a natural reaction for Delaney to stand up. A woman's voice gently soothed Delaney's heart with melodic whispers. The voice was that of her teacher, Mrs. Hughes. *How was it possible? Where did she come from? Am I imagining it?* thought Delaney. Mrs. Hughes' sweet, soothing voice seemed shallow and echoed, but Delaney could detect the love. Mrs. Hughes encouraged her to prepare herself to walk away. Mrs. Hughes promised to walk with her. Delaney slightly shook her head in agreement. With each step leading her further away from her dead father's body, she kept her focus on the ground. Delaney felt her own humanness somehow leak out of her, leaving only a shell of a person.

They had taken only a few steps when Delaney paused and turned to Mrs. Hughes. She asked, "What time is it?"

Confused, Mrs. Hughes responded, "What? It's 4:15." Delaney took a deep breath to steady herself. Mrs. Hughes could see the wheels turning in this young girl's head but wasn't sure she was equipped to help. Claire is still kneeling on the ground in a puddle of anguish. Delaney looks back towards her and then back to the bystanders. She asks a man, "What day is it?" She had actually forgotten the date and, in her scrambled mind, couldn't figure it out.

She raised herself up to stand a little taller and intuitively knew that she was forever changed. The world looked a little less colorful and a bit blurry as if she needed glasses. People moved in slow motion, or maybe it was only her moving slowly. She went from feeling immense pain in her innermost being to feeling absolutely nothing at all. Delaney looked down on her mother, laying undignified over her father's lifeless body while Claire's was alive, riving in pain. Others tried to console her mother, but it was no use.

Delaney, wiping away her own tears, stepped back towards her mother and said, "Momma, can you hear me?" Claire looked strangely at Delaney as if she didn't know why she was responding or what effect this little girl's voice had on her. She simply nodded yes. Delaney added, "Momma, Daddy departed at 4:15 on April 15. He would say 'That's right on time.' I think God made a big mistake today, but it doesn't matter now. We need to go home now, Momma." Delaney wrapped her small, wiry arms around her mother and gently pulled her upwards as Mrs. Hughes had done for her. Claire responded like a small child willing to go where directed.

As her mother rose, Delaney glanced around to see where to go next, and a lightning bolt of shock went through her as she recognized the graffitied boxcar that had plagued her day. It was the culprit of her father's death. She looked at the train car and released her mother's care to Mrs. Hughes. She walked in its direction, stood directly in front of the car, and without the fear of judgment, undignifiedly screamed, "You stole his life! I will not shed another tear because of you. I double dare you to take mine too. The sooner, the better." She picks up the only rock she can find at her feet and, with all her might, throws it at the cursed car. With resolve on her face, Delaney turns around, resumes her mother's care, and begins walking towards home as the crowd parts before her.

This morning, the words "Stolen Lives" were a confusing, menacing message, but now, it was crystal clear and finite. At least one life was stolen today, and in a weird way, she felt comfort in knowing it had been acknowledged for what it was, a cruel, greedy act of desperation. It wasn't an accident but rather a life plucked from this earth at its prime and without cause. Delaney was numb and lifeless. She had witnessed her mother's heart so rattled that it is doubtful the pieces would ever fit back together.

One thought overwhelmed Delaney: who's to blame? This question made her spirit shake and spin. She couldn't even conceive of an answer, so she pushed it out as fast as it came in. There would be a time for that later, but she knew she would surely blame someone.

As you stand in this scene, you are enamored by this young girl. You have seen a transformation in her but aren't sure if it is for better or worse. You look for the Creators. Where are they now? Are there any other eternals? You know there must be, but you seem to be the only one at the moment. As you contemplate the scene, you feel that time is drawing to a close on this car. You trust that you have learned all you need to and accept that it is time to move on. As you blink, your eyelids seem to rest one on top of the other for a pause that brings great sweetness and rest. It must be longer than a blink, but you aren't sure how long. As your eyes open, you are fully engaged with the new location and continuation of Delaney's amazing story.

CHAPTER 5

THIS HOUSE DELANEY ONCE LOVED so much makes her feel like a trapped animal. Its walls close in on her, and she feels like it is getting smaller, dirtier, and dingier every day. The sun doesn't come through the windows anymore, and the sound of silence is deafening. Kinsley and her mother are simple creatures who rarely venture outside. They find solace in staying home where it is safe and predictable. Delaney doesn't understand their bond or when it formed. It seems like they found comfort in one another and don't need anything or anyone else. She remembers a time when she and Kinsley could almost breathe for each other, but now it seems they are barely breathing at all. Delaney feels compelled to gasp enough air in every breath to sustain them all. If she doesn't, who will?

A train whistle can be heard far into the distance on its early morning conquest, and Kinsley looks across the room to catch Delaney's eyes in the dark room. She was hoping one day they would jump out of bed and run to the train as they had done in the happier years, but she wasn't surprised to see Delaney with glassy eyes and a deadpan face staring back at her. Ever since *that day*, there were no celebratory traditions in their home, only sad rituals to remember the saddest day of their lives. Kinsley could tell that Delaney wasn't in the mood, so she rolled back over and decided it best to pretend to be asleep. Oh, how Kinsley hoped for more, but she knew Delaney's heart couldn't take it, so they continued living with heavy sadness in the atmosphere.

Delaney detests the sound of the train rattling through her bones; it is far worse on this day of all days. No one acknowledges the deafening sound because, in order to survive the pain, the birthday tradition had to die with Dennis. After several failed, internal commands, Delaney counts to three and makes herself get out of bed and slide into the most convenient jeans laying on the floor and sweater draped over the footboard. She is on autopilot and with minimal effort, manages to pull her naturally thick, wavy hair into a ponytail. Her complexion was flawless and didn't require much make-up. Her bright blue eyes were her best feature and the only thing about herself that she tolerated.

As Delaney makes her way downstairs, it is as she predicted. She is the first one awake in this lonely house and recognizes the symbolism of the moment. She gathers the typical ingredients and begins making her own birthday breakfast minus the smiley face pancakes. After some time, she hears Momma's slippers shuffling across the dirty wooden floor and feels a gentle hug around her shoulders. She knows it should feel good, but it makes her cringe with dissatisfaction. As Kinsley makes her way downstairs, they all sit in their normal places, leaving an empty seat for her dead father, a tradition she wished had never started but doesn't know how to stop.

Kinsley and her mother look sweetly at Delaney, excited for her to realize there is a neatly wrapped package laid out for her discovery. Delaney sees the package but doesn't want to accept that it is real. She understands that whatever it is, it isn't worth the expense. They didn't have a penny to spare; in the end, it would be a present she unintentionally bought herself with the overtime she would work this week to make up the difference.

Kinsley says, "Won't you open it?"

Delaney sighs inside, then allows a smile to unfold on the outside. "What in the world have you done? Thank you so much for remembering me." It was all she could muster, but after hearing it come out, she felt satisfied that it sounded authentic and possibly upbeat. Everything she does nowadays feels like she is a robot living underwater. She feels resistance when walking, talking takes her breath away, responses are programmed, and listening is filtered. She cannot get free of the funk surrounding her.

As she opens the package, her brain thinks it knows what it is, but the words are scrambled. The montage of images rapidly flash before her to the point she isn't sure if she is remembering it or making it up. Her focus settles on one image of a watch once resting on her father's wrist. Could it be? How do they have it? Wouldn't it be on his dead, cold body six feet in the ground? Who took it off? Why now? Where has it been?

Sensing her confusion, Delaney's mother reaches over and places her hand on top of hers. "Your father would have wanted you to have it," she says. "We never had a lot, but Gramps gave your father this watch when he graduated from high school, and he wore it every single day. It doesn't work anymore but probably just needs a new battery." Delaney looked at the black band with its worn edges and wondered how it still stayed together. The white face with its classic roman numerals was a familiar and oddly comforting sight. Time stood still at 8:15. She found it a curiosity. When had it stopped? Before or after he died? Without thinking, she placed it over her wrist and latched the backside. She adjusted the time to 4:15 and the date to April 15. It felt eerie, but at least it was a feeling. For the first time in five years, she felt something and had a connection back to him.

Kinsley knew she had done well. Although there weren't accolades, tears of happiness, or even a hug, the gift had reached deep down into her sister and managed to pull out a nano-glimpse of the one within, true and familiar. It was *that* sister Kinsley longed for, and even if it weren't possible to have her back fully, she was proud of being able to touch her soul even for a fleeting moment.

CHAPTER 6

D ELANEY WALKS AWAY from the house and gets into a car
parked a couple of streets away. She prefers that Claire and
Kinsley not be in her business. Randy, a twenty-year-old man with
cheap tattoos and long sideburns, is waiting for Delaney in his used
Chevy truck. Randy graduated a few years back and is a super senior
still hanging around their sleepy town, trying to create some glory
days that never transpired the first time around.

Delaney met Randy through friends while doing the drag through
town on a Saturday night. He didn't know she was only fifteen when
they met, which bothered him a little, but he got over it quickly
because of how mature she acted. She was decisive, beautiful, and
knew what she wanted, and as long as it was him, he was good with
it. Randy was unsure about Delaney. She was a walking contradiction
and it sometimes scared him. She was popular, everyone knew her
in town, and definitely the teacher's pet. She was also wild, unpredictable, and independent. When she walked into a room, everyone
knew it. Not because she was the bubbly extravert full of optimism,
but because she commanded it, on guard and ready for anything.

Randy is smoking a cigarette, leaning against the passenger door.
As Delaney approaches his truck, Randy, as usual, grabs hold of
her ass, claiming his territory. He proudly says, "Hey, birthday girl!
Gotta present for me?" Then he laughs at his own unoriginal humor.

Delaney, without any fanfare, replies, "Yep… I'm pregnant."

Randy thinks she is joking, then looks at her stoic expression and
suddenly realizes she's not. He says, "Wait, what? No way. What the
hell? Wait, that's how you tell me? Are you sure? When?"

Delaney pulls a pregnancy test from inside her bra and then sarcastically says, "Pretty sure. The double blue line says I'm the winner."

Randy, still slightly confused, says, "Oh, wow. I mean…" He runs his hands through his own hair and paces back and forth, letting it sink in. He tries to console Delaney by reaching for a strand of hair that has fallen out of her ponytail. Delaney rejects his efforts. Randy asserts himself by saying, "I'm here for you. We'll figure this out. Does anyone else know?"

Delaney looks at him, and the absurdity of this moment is not lost on her. She sighs, then says, "Are you kidding? No way, and that's the way it's gonna stay. Look, I've thought about it, and I'm having an abortion. I need you to give me the money to do it."

Randy pauses to think, stares into her cold, blue eyes, and says, "Yea. Okay, I mean, if that's what you want. I'm not sure how I feel about it."

Delaney seems resolved and says, "It doesn't matter what you think, really. I'm the one who's pregnant, and it's my life that's totally fucked up, and the last thing I need is a baby."

Randy can tell by looking at her that there will absolutely be no changing her mind, but he proceeds anyways, "Have you thought about getting married or something like that? I mean, I have a job now, and my grandmother would let us live with her."

Delaney giggles sarcastically, "Me? Married. I'm only fifteen! That would really be 'making my life matter,' wouldn't it?"

Randy is confused by the "making my life matter" comment. She says it when she is mad, and it has never made sense to him. He responded honestly, "I don't know. It just seems like something to consider. Why do you always say shit about 'Making your life matter' and stuff? What does that even mean?"

Delaney fidgets with the cassette player and picks other cassettes from a case. It seems like she isn't listening but that's not unusual for her. Randy raises his voice and says, "Hey, look at me." Delaney stops and looks at him. She is fragile but trying to act strong. Randy continues, "You scare me sometimes. You somehow seem like an old woman, and I don't get it."

Delaney is agitated and responds, "You would never understand; I don't understand me." Decisively, she commands, "I'm going to be late; take me to school."

Randy asks, "That's it? End of discussion?"

Delaney says, "What's there to discuss? My mom would kill me. My sister would hate me. My life would be over; everyone thinks you are too old and I am too young. I reckon it's the right thing to do."

Randy shrugs in agreement because she sums it up exactly as he sees it too. He starts the car, and they drive off.

As the car makes its way down the familiar, dusty roads, you get the sense that you have learned all you need to, and light pulls itself away from the moment and travels behind you to a new place. You watch the scene grow darker and darker. You haven't had your fill, but you know it is time to move forward. As you turn around to follow the light, you are propelled forward in its leading.

CHAPTER 7

DELANEY CAN'T BELIEVE she found herself in this God-forsaken place again. The grey, sterile walls are filled with overly cheerful people who say comforting words but look at her with daggers of judgment. The last time she was here, everyone tried to convince her she was making the right decision. Justifications ran from "She was too young to have a baby" to "The pregnancy was so new, it wasn't really a baby yet," then "millions of women had made this choice before her, and they were glad they gained their lives back." She didn't expect it to be pain-free, but she wasn't prepared for the constant feeling that she had carved out a literal piece of herself, and it was forever gone. She felt a hole in her womb and wondered if an infection had set in because she seemed to stink with shame. She was disgusted with herself and wanted to die. All that ran through her mind was, "You stupid girl!"

At least, this time, Delaney knew what to expect. As Kinsley sits beside her sister, she tries to hold Delaney's hand, but Delaney withdrawals it and is obviously feeling unworthy of Kinsley's love. Kinsley reassures Delaney, "It's going to be okay, D. We'll get through it together." Delaney is staring off into space. Everything has changed. They were lost in a current of life, taking them further and further away from a place of security they once had in each other. They longed to feel again, but after their father's death, Delaney went numb, and Kinsley was desperate for connection.

After a long pause, she responds, "How the hell did I end up here again?" It registers on Kinsley's face that Delaney just admitted to this being a second abortion. Delaney can read her sister's reaction without even looking at her, "It's true. I can't even imagine what you think of your Big Sis now." Kinsley knows that it's best to leave Delaney to herself in moments like this and not try to ask questions, hug her, or do anything. Delaney, still a little despondent, says, "The smell of this place is still in my nose from the last time. I am forever stained with death's scent." Delaney makes a scrubbing motion on her arms, and Kinsley doesn't know if she is cold or trying to shake off the shame. Kinsley doesn't know what to do or say and feels as if she is invisible. Delaney always does things on her own and without anyone's help. She didn't guess this would be any different, but she hoped.

A nurse appears. "Delaney?"

Delaney finishes the inquiry in her head with the definition "Killer." As she makes this silent proclamation, she cringes and feels nauseated. She tries to stand, but her knees buckle, and she sits back down in her chair. She commands her body to stand, but it just won't move. She wasn't sure that her legs could hold the weight of her heavy heart if she made it to her feet. Kinsley helps her to stand, but it is difficult. When she tries to take a step forward, it is almost impossible. The weight of the atmosphere was tangible, and when she finally walked forward, the room transformed as if she were in a dirty tank of water, she couldn't breathe. After a few feet, the nurse comes to her and calls for help. Together, they walk her to a room and ask Kinsley to wait outside. Delaney nods in agreement as she is escorted out of sight.

Kinsley reluctantly sits back down in the waiting room. She is feeling uncomfortable, cold and has a strong disdain for the environment. Because Delaney pointed it out, Kinsley tucks her chin and nose in her shirt because of the indescribable, odd smell that fills this place and begins to softly cry.

The nurse helps Delaney undress. Her mind had disconnected from what was really happening as if she had crawled inside herself into a tiny, dark closet tucked away in her mind. She hears them talking, but it is like listening to a conversation underwater. They put her on the exam table and placed both feet into stirrups. She cannot get the smell of death out of her nose. The smell is all around her and emanates from the trash cans, drawers, under the door, and the nurses' bodies. She covers her nose, trying to keep it from getting into her body.

The doctor comes into the room, and he carries the rotting smell of death with him. He nods to talk to Delaney. She agrees as if she knows what they are saying, but her mind is jumbled, and she isn't comprehending and doesn't care. For some strange reason, the memory of her twelfth birthday and her father's expression of love popped into her mind when he looked at her on their front porch. She was glad he wasn't here to see her murdering another baby. He would be ashamed of her creating a baby she had absolutely no capacity to love. Delaney rambles to herself, "C'mon, Delaney. You've been here before and survived. Thank God Dad isn't here to see this. He's lucky he's dead because if he knew me like this, it'd definitely kill him. Shit! Don't worry about what God is thinking. There's no way he is here. The smell. God, the smell. Death." Delaney shutters as every nerve in her body contracts and releases from her feet to her head. She wants to peel her skin back and run away from here.

Her legs are parted and held back. As the instrument is inserted into her, she feels a violent, cold abdominal cramp; she understands this baby is being dismantled inside her. In her imagination, she saw the little round window of a laundromat machine with a baby in dirty water being tossed around. She knew she wouldn't save it but hoped its doomed fate would come to an end quickly. *Die quick. Go ahead. Drown. Hurry up,* she thought, and then she felt it. Like last time, a searing pain inside her started down low and found its destructive way up through her body, her broken heart, and like a bolt of lightning into her brain, dismantling her thoughts. Before she could recover, she heard a train whistle, enough to send her over the ledge. It was too much. She involuntarily let out a blood-curdling scream that shook her to the core and scared even her. It was from another place and was full of terror, sorrow, and shame. With crazy eyes, she looked at the nurses and the doctor and said, "Where did that train come from? Why is there a train in here? Where is the train?"

The nurses exchanged glances that Delaney saw on both their faces. The nurse responded, "It's okay, Delaney. You're going to be okay. There aren't any trains in this town. We don't have any train tracks or train stations. You're just feeling a little frazzled at the moment. The worst is over."

Delaney couldn't believe what she was hearing. She looked at the nurses and said, "Don't make me feel crazy. I'm not crazy. I heard a train. It's coming for me, it's coming for you, and It's coming for us all, straight from hell."

The nurse said to the doctor as if Delaney wasn't present, "Have you ever seen anything like that? What just happened?"

The doctor commented, "I thought you said she's had one before."

Delaney can hear them talking about her, but she is fixated on the clock on the wall. It is 10:15. Her mind is racing yet strangely stuck in one place.

The conversation continues with the nurse answering, "She has; I don't know what just happened. I didn't see that coming."

Delaney despondently verbalizes the realization in her head, Oh, my God… A stolen life."

The doctor asks, "What's that?"

Delaney clarifies, "Stolen life, times two. Lives that don't really matter, right doc?"

The doctor is confused and looks at the nurse. He recognizes that Delaney's strength is beyond her years; even though he doesn't understand, her words are sobering. He would have no answer for her and wonders if it was a question at all. The nurses aren't inclined to console her either. Truth be told, they are a little afraid of her and work efficiently to quickly wrap this session up.

As Delaney slowly gets dressed, she sees glitter on the back of her hand, then notices it on her other arm and on the lens of her father's watch. She touches it, and it rubs off on her fingers; then, she rolls the glitter around on her fingertips. When she looks at the glitter, it is fine and beautiful. The color is gold yet iridescent, unlike anything she has seen before. She is convinced she is imagining it and has probably lost her mind with full-blown hallucinations. She looks into a mirror on the wall and says to herself, *C'mon! You've got this. This isn't a good time to go crazy.* After a long sigh and looking at the glitter again, "If I'm crazy, I might as well hallucinate glitter," she laughs sarcastically.

Delaney walks out of the dingy, grey examination room and down the long hall to go home. When she exits the waiting room, Kinsley stands to greet her with a look of genuine relief and moves toward her. Kinsley, looking curious, says, "Hey Sis, how are you?" Kinsley is taken aback by how Delaney looks refreshed and almost glowing. She wonders how Delaney could have gone through something like this but still look composed and strong. Kinsley notices the glitter all over Delaney and asks, "Where did this come from? What is it? It looks like glitter, but different." It registers with Delaney that Kinsley actually sees this glitter and that it isn't a figment of her imagination.

Relieved, Delaney asks, "Do you see it too?"

Kinsley laughs, "Yes, silly. Of course, where did you get it?"

Delaney answered, "I… I didn't. I mean, it just appeared." Kinsley shrugs her shoulders, happy for a more lighthearted moment.

As they leave the clinic, Delaney stops dead in her tracks. She changes the time on her dad's watch to say 10:15. As she does, images flash in her mind like an invasive movie she is being forced to watch; her own birth at 3:03, her dying father at 4:15, the first abortion at 2:20 and now this monstrosity of a moment at 10:15. These times are seared into her soul as monuments, markers in time.

You are overwhelmed by the depth of Delaney's pain. Her story is unique to her but it resonates with your own experience. You long to rewrite her life story and can see how she was shaped by the circumstances of her twelfth birthday. If you could, how would things have changed? As your mind wonders, you are pulled back out of this scene slowly and steadily. You have a bird's eye view of the clinic, the street, the block, the city, and now the whole region of West Texas. You are keenly aware there are no railroad tracks within view. What then did she hear during the procedure?

CHAPTER 8

S HE SCORED BIG THIS TIME! Finally. A little bit of happiness. James always seemed to catch Delaney's eye and was the one person that made her feel something. She always found it strange that such a vivacious, passionate athlete would create crowd-consuming drama on the baseball diamond but privately seek out quiet, solitude, and simplicity. It was as if he were two different people. She wasn't entirely sure what made him tick but felt a personal connection with him of having two very distinct sides. She learned to be cordial to others, smiling when they talked, looking sincerely into their eyes, nodding, and preparing her engaging comeback to their maddening conversation. Being idyllic was easier than entertaining their well-meaning but super-irritating concerns. James was the same. He was short and to the point with others, and they respected him for it. She found it mildly irritating how people let him be reserved but weren't satisfied when she tried to do the same.

Tonight, was like all the rest. They sat on the tailgate of his truck at the top of the bluff overlooking the lake on a dark, starry night. The world seemed to fall asleep easily, and they were glad for it. In the expanse of the night, she wondered if her father saw her here, a teeny tiny little person in this very big world. Sitting in silence with James was peaceful. She didn't know what ran through his head in these moments but had zero inclination to find out. Carrying any of his burdens wasn't a pastime she would indulge in.

While looking out over the moon's reflection on the water, he casually said, "You know what? I think you're the only person I really like."

Delaney laughed because she had the same thoughts from time to time. She responded, "That's good because I'm the only person around." He seemed so preoccupied in his own mind, Delaney thought.

James turned to her without moving any other part of his body beside his head and simply said, "Will you marry me?"

Delaney would have laughed out loud, except his expression was so serious. The flashbacks came fast and furious of every moment they had spent together, simple times doing simple things, her comfort with him, and the fact that she had no reasonable objection. He was respected in their small town, and even though she had never told him her past, the grapevine was a well-oiled machine, and he didn't seem to look at her with pity, so he either didn't know the details or didn't care. She was okay with either one. As the imaginary timer went off in her head, indicating a decision must be made, she naturally said, "Yes."

An expression of relief consumed his face, and it surprised her. Did he really think she would say no? Did he think she had a lot of options? She knew in her heart that this was the best possible outcome for her. He would respect her inner shell, and she would do the same for him.

She knew the routine… nausea, barf, cold rag on the forehead, repeat daily. This time, pregnancy didn't feel like an impossible, out of control train on the tracks to nowhere but rather a new adventure. Delaney's heart seemed so much softer now. James was as kind as she had hoped. She felt more herself and could laugh without stabbing pains of guilt. He truly loved her and respected her need for privacy. The more space he gave, the closer she inched in. The thought of having his child growing in her felt like a secret worth keeping safe from the rest of the world. This perfect little bundle was a chance to start new and fresh, and the innocence of this life would be something she would give every one of her heartbeats and breath to make sure she nurtured. This secret joy would erase secret sorrow pushed way down deep.

Immediately, the thought of her own father looking into her eyes on the front porch of that fateful day became very clear. He looked at her as a secret joy. His secret love for her was beyond anything she had ever known, and he couldn't have explained it even if he tried. It was bigger than the stories. Bigger than the lessons. His future was wrapped up in his family, and now, she would secretly vow to him to do right by this child, "Daddy. I'm pregnant. I have a little one of my own, and although you probably already know about my others, I know you are going to help me love this one with my whole heart." Taking a deep sigh, she continued, "It just feels right this time. This isn't a mistake. This child has already healed my hurt, and it will do the same for James. I'm not sure what he will say when I tell him, but I think he will feel the same. Life is so strange. Some twists and turns can't be expected, and I guess we all do have a purpose like you always said. This baby will arrive right on time, and the world needs him or her. My time may be over, but this baby will do something big. I just know it!" The atmosphere seemed to shift, and she felt like an observer in her own conversation. She made fun of herself and smirked a bit, thinking it was silly to talk to thin air, but then, just as suddenly, she corrected herself and said, "No. Daddy, I know you are here. Please watch over us. Tell me what I need to know to not screw this up. I trust you."

Just as Delaney finished her conversation with her father, James entered the room and leaned against the door seal. He had a strange and oddly peaceful look on his face. When Delaney turned towards him, she asked, "What's up? Why are you looking at me funny?"

Still looking a little strange, he smiled slightly and said, "You're so beautiful Delaney. I just don't get tired of looking at you."

Delaney replied, "Well, you might when my belly gets to poking out to here, and I weigh three hundred pounds." James looked confused, but then Delaney stood up, supported her arched back with both hands, and poked out her flat stomach to mimic a woman about to give birth.

He said, "What! Are you pregnant?"

She smiled and simply said, "Yes."

The smile on James' face grew wider and wider as the realization sunk in. His normally calm, collected demeanor went right out the door then he let out a big "Whoop" as he rushed to pick Delaney up and sling her around. Delaney was so happy in this moment. Wrongs really were right; it felt like not just a new day but a new life for all of them.

CHAPTER 9

T HE PREGNANCY could only be described as blissful. Delaney and James were as poor as church mice, but they didn't notice it. As an aunt once told them, they were "Living off love" and didn't need much else. James' job wasn't much, but it was steady and allowed him to provide for Delaney. She was a great budgeter and didn't spend anything beyond what was allowed in her meticulous envelope system. Delaney found an excellent job with the school district and had found a passion for working with special education children. People commented how patient she was with them and that she noticed every person as a valued, special individual and never let someone go overlooked on her watch. She had abounding ideas on ways to engage her students, and they trusted her explicitly because they could tell she deeply cared for them. It was a relief to be with her students because they knew her in a way that most didn't. Her walls were down because they had none. There was no reason to protect herself when in their presence. She knew them in a way that was different from everyone else and appreciated their old souls no matter what their outward appearance presented.

She was only a week away from her due date when her water broke at work. It was a frenzy as administration, teachers, and even students were jockeying for position to take her to the hospital. She calmly called James, and he came within minutes to get her. They were beyond excited as they approached the hospital. She had thought through this so often that it seemed more like a past memory than one in the present.

Giving birth and the associated pain felt almost like a relief. It was payback for not having gone through it with her other children. As every wave came upon her, she took it as penitence to be paid. "Right the wrong, right the wrong, right the wrong" was her internal dialog. The nurses complimented Delaney on her ability to focus. She relished the whole experience and considered it a great honor. The pain didn't bother her because she understood it and knew it was temporary. Emotional pain was a much bigger enemy because it crept up on her and caught her by surprise, over and over again.

Delaney and James welcomed their beautiful baby boy into the world with one last push. She stared at the clock directly over the doctor's head because she didn't want to miss the exact time of birth. Her father's watch was on her wrist as it had been for years, and she intended to remember this epic moment in time. Taven James was born at 4:15 in the morning, and it felt perfectly on time. Later she would marvel that it was twelve hours to the minute before her father died. Somehow it seemed fitting.

She breathed a sigh of relief as she heard the baby's cry and watched the nurse work frantically to prepare him for her to hold. As he was nestled onto her chest, she stopped breathing as she looked into his big, beautiful, sky-blue eyes as round as silver dollars. His soul was old and instantly connected to hers. She looked at him and wondered how someone so fresh from God could be at home in her arms. His eyes entranced hers, and then she knew. Taven had her and her father's eyes. It was as if Dennis was staring back at her, and it made her wonder.

The trance was broken by the busyness of the moment. James wrapped his arms around her, kissed her forehead, and marveled at this tiny miracle. Without saying a word, they both wondered how they deserved such a perfect gift; then Delaney asked James to take the watch off her wrist. He wasn't sure what all this was about, the watch and all. When he asked before, she would sidestep it. As he unlatched it, she continued to admire her new baby and simply said,

"Can you set the time to 4:15, please?" James looked at the clock and corrected her to say it was actually 5:03. She kindly looked at him and said, "I know, but I want it set to 4:15." He also noticed that it wasn't keeping time but didn't want to ruin the moment, so he kept quiet. The name they had chosen, Taven, was a perfect fit for this precious one.

After months at home, Delaney fell into the routine of motherhood as if she had done it a dozen times before. She often thought that she would have made a terrific pioneer woman. She could make something out of nothing and always had her baby at her side while getting in a full day's work. Everyone commented on how happy she had been. Claire marveled at how this baby had made Delaney so playful and childlike. She missed seeing her daughter this way, and it reminded her of the good times when her little ones sang and danced above her room in that small house next to the tracks. She would sometimes wonder if the ceiling would cave in! It sounds odd, but it was almost as if Delaney and Taven were growing up together and discovering the beauty of the world around them.

Claire wondered if she just imagined it, but it seemed to her Taven was a very compliant baby. He never cried, slept through the night, and never indicated discomfort. Her girls had never been that way, and she told herself not to worry. She reassured herself that Taven must get it from James' family. Delaney and James were both mature and calm for their young age, and the house was rather quiet; but still, she had a nagging feeling that something might be wrong. Whenever she thought of bringing it up, she would rationalize to herself that she was over worrying and making up problems. Being a "worry wort" was a trait she had been accused of for many years. She felt it best to keep it to herself and continue to watch.

On a beautiful day playing in the park, Claire finally made the simple suggestion that Taven seemed more relaxed and less engaged in comparison to other children his age. Claire's observation became an icepick-sized hole in Delaney's heart open to a small but steady flow of fear. Delaney prayed that the "worry cycle" wouldn't come back. When her past came at her, she worried that things were going so well that it was time for a cosmic payback from God. She quickly filed her mother's suggestion away in the back storeroom of her mind hoping to be hidden from herself and the world forever; but even the mention of it carried a real feeling of dread eroding at her beautiful life.

As Taven became older, she noticed that his physical ability to play with other kids started with bursts of enthusiasm and energy, but it wouldn't be long until he would leave his friends to come and sit by Delaney's side. After a rest, he would rejoin them but never with as much energy. It was like he ran on batteries that depleted quickly. Delaney dreaded the conversations she was having with herself throughout the day and made an appointment with the pediatrician to hopefully stop the chatter in her head.

Hoping for the best, Delaney took Taven to the various tests that were recommended after a series of appointments, but she could tell there was a shroud of secrecy at each appointment by well-meaning health professionals. She was oddly grateful to have them participate in her denial just a little while longer. If only they knew about her past, she was sure they would feel less inclined to treat her with kindness.

The day did finally come when an extremely intelligent doctor and his nurse arranged an appointment to discuss the results. Delaney, Claire, and Kinsley sat in his sterile office to receive the news that Taven had an autoimmune disease that would require a lifetime of transfusions and hospital visits. His life expectancy was less than twenty years, and the medical team were eager to begin treatment and caregiver education. Delaney's mind was spinning out of control, and she wanted to break down into a million little pieces, but she couldn't. She was so afraid of losing all her pieces, never to be found, and who would take care of Taven? Her mother and sister were devastated by the news and it was hard to tell who had been hit the hardest. All she could see was the mental image of that ugly train car from so many years ago. Another stolen life has been added to its hit list. She silently prayed to God to let the next extinguished life be her own and not her precious child.

Delaney knew bargaining with God was of no use and talking to her father was probably nonsense. She would have to pull up her own bootstraps and forge her way through the now gushing hole in her heart to take care of her son. She regretted not having James take off work for this appointment. She convinced him it would be a good report, and her mother and sister were available so she would have support. But, in reality, everything just changed, and James wasn't present for the pivot that had uncontrollably taken place. She was on her own, and walking it alone felt like a terrible calling but one she had instantly resided herself to. As she composed herself, she stood up and walked like a zombie to the car, putting every file in her brain back into place and securing the storeroom of emotions with a padlock. Her mother and sister would have to be the ones to express the hurt because she was determined to set it aside forever.

As she reached the car and buckled Taven in his car seat, she smelled the most delightful scent. It was unlike anything she had ever smelled, especially in a hospital parking garage! It was a beautiful, clean flower smell but more fragrant than an actual flower or perfume. She asked if anyone else smelled it, and they said they didn't, but then Taven innocently said, "You smell good, Mommy," and with a long, dramatic breath, he took it all in. Delaney smelled it too, and she was satisfied knowing it was a secret experience for just the two of them.

Day by day, the treatments dragged on, and the reality of this being their new life had set in. Delaney felt her experience at the school prepared her for small victories and finding ways to connect and appreciate the tiniest wins. James, however, just couldn't accept this new reality. He was working every shift he could pick up, but the bills were coming in faster than he could wake up to a day's pay. He

missed everything, the good and the bad. Every doctor's appointment, the treatments, a precious smile, and even late-night vomits
and diaper changes. Delaney wouldn't let anyone take care of Taven,
which he understood, but he could see there was a divide growing
between him and them. Feeling excluded opened up an old wound,
and James isolated himself as a preemptive measure. He took on the
role of money manager and was failing at that too.

One evening, they fought fiercely over something so trivial neither
one would be able to remember it, but their ability to hurt each other
had raised to an Olympic standard. This night, James took his coat
and keys, looked Delaney in the eyes, and with tears streaming down
his face, he said, "I have managed to love you more than I have loved
anyone. I did my best to provide for you and Taven, but I can see
in your eyes that I am not enough and will never be enough. You
are always talking about our destiny and having a purpose, but I'm
telling you right now, this isn't it. I'm not like you. I'm not made for
this. If I don't get out now, I'll never be able to breathe, and what
kind of father would that be? I'm dying on the inside."

Delaney tried to stop him because she could tell he was about to
say something they would both regret, but he continued, "I'm filing
for divorce. I'll send you whatever money I can, but I can't do this
any longer." Tears ran down his face in stark contrast to his actions.
As he turned to walk out the door, Delaney ran after him and begged
him not to leave. She apologized, but he got in his car, and as he drove
off, she knew in her gut that he was gone. He was as much gone as
if he had died that day, and she knew she was forever on her own.

She walked back inside the house and went straight to Taven's
room. She was amazed he could sleep through all that racket. She
looked up, closed her eyes, and asked, "God, are you real? Are you out
there? This would be a good time to show up if you are." She switched
gears and said, "Daddy, I need your help to raise this child. Please
help me." As she started to walk away from the crib, she glanced back
to check Taven's breathing and noticed what seemed to be gold dust

resting on his little cheek. She touched it and immediately remembered the gold dust she saw at the abortion clinic. She thought to
herself, *How strange.* Instead of feeling like she was hallucinating or
going crazy, this time, she just accepted it as a mystery and appreciated the special moment. As she shut the door to the nursery, she
knew her life had switched tracks yet another time.

CHAPTER 10

L IFE WITH A SICK CHILD was a constant state of fatigue, and although it was difficult, she knew not to diminish a single day. Every day was a gift, and she had purposed in her heart to not become bitter towards this child but to live out each moment. She didn't think it was possible, but she had come to a place where she was thankful for at least one life lesson that had come from her father's death. Everyone always told her, "Things happen for a reason," and every time she heard it, she wanted to punch them out cold. Maybe it was years of being tired or having cried so much; her anger had gone with it, and she had come to accept that life is short, and any time we have together is a privilege. She wasn't to the point of "thanking God" for it all and certainly not for Taven's sickness, but she found a sliver of peace in the life the two of them had carved out. James was around, but he always kept his distance. She assumed he was trying to protect his heart. Delaney didn't mind because it kept things simple. Taven knew he had a daddy who loved him, and James didn't complicate things or get in the way. Taven wasn't old enough yet to be disappointed in his father, which was a relief to Delaney. She worked hard to be enough for them both.

Delaney lived in contentment. She had Taven, and even though there were daily rituals of prescriptions, medical dos and don'ts, and a constant cloud of fear, she had accepted it as a new normal and wanted to provide a life for her son that was full of love, friends, and family. Her relationship with her mother and sister had healed, and she no longer felt the anger she once had watching them move on after her father's death.

She thought for many years that it was her duty to stay strong, make the decisions, and lead their family in his absence. She took that vow seriously when she cursed the train car and dared it to steal another life. She fought hard to protect herself and others with her wall of hatred, but it became too much, even for her. James had given her a sliver of hope with his quiet disposition and easy acceptance of her body, mind, and soul. Then, together, they created a masterpiece in Taven, and instead of hating God for his illness, she decided she needed His healing power more than her own need for revenge. Years ago at 4:15 AM in a hospital maternity ward, she looked into Tavens eyes and vowed to seek goodness and mercy for this child. She had never forgotten it.

Without seeking it, Delaney attracted men's attention, but she didn't have any need for it. She was beautiful and engaging, but dealing with a man wasn't even up for discussion. She had two loving women in her life that she could count on, and although James was a good man, he was weak and unable to handle the tougher times in life. Not having to baby him was a relief, and she had more than once thanked God for clearing out the clutter so she could be better equipped to focus on Taven.

She didn't notice Beckett for months even though he creatively found ways to see her at church, at the gas station, and worked to find friends in common. He popped up everywhere, but it never occurred to her that he had an interest in her. He was handsome, established, raising two kids of his own, and seasoned by heartache. She quickly learned not to mistake his soft-spoken nature as a weakness. He was strong, decisive, and morally steady. On their first date, she knew she was in trouble. He might actually be 'the one', she thought.

Delaney's instincts were right, and almost immediately, they dreamed of building a future together. He loved Taven like his own, and his children accepted her not as their mother but as a very good friend which was exactly as she had hoped. She was grateful for the relationship and found Beckett to be a counterbalance she had never known. She had resolved within herself not to have any more children because she worried the same genetic disorder would befall other children, and she had righted her wrongs with Taven and didn't want to undo it with a careless decision. Beckett had spoken early in their relationship that he wanted to have more children with her. Delaney recorded it in her internal log and decided that he would be an amazing friend for now, but it couldn't be a long-term relationship because of the difference in opinion on having a baby.

Beckett proposed, and Delaney respectfully declined because she wanted him to have the life he had dreamed of, and she wasn't willing to take any chances. Beckett had a way of getting the real story out of her. He opened her up in ways no one ever had, and when she admitted to her fear of having other sick children, he convinced her to seek genetic counseling together before making a final decision.

They sat with a doctor at the finest children's hospital in the United States and nervously prepared for the verdict. In his cluttered office, Delaney noticed every detail of the room. There were so many files and books that she wondered if he had read them or if they were there for show. He opened their file, and Beckett took her hand. The doctor painstakingly reviewed their files, and although he spoke directly to them, Delaney heard it as if it were underwater and thought, *Why does this always happen to me? What is he saying?* She couldn't take it any longer and interrupted the doctor, "Excuse me, but what is your final decision? If we were to have children, what would the chances be of us having another child with Taven's same condition?"

The doctor understood this look and tone well. Delaney needed a clear answer, so he looked her in the eyes and said, "Statistically, there is zero probability that your children would have the same condition." He added, "Taven's condition is extremely rare, and having two children in the same family and with different fathers would not be impossible but very unlikely."

Delaney confirmed for her own peace of mind, "So, you are saying that we could have a baby together and it would be healthy or at least not have Taven's condition?" As the doctor nodded yes, Beckett leaned over to hug Delaney, who turned to him with tears in her eyes and said, "I will marry you, Beckett. You are the love of my life. I love you more than I ever hoped or dreamed for. I love you and the way you love everyone around you. Please spend your life with me."

Beckett wrapped himself around her and held tight to this woman. She was his future, and he embraced her with all he had.

CHAPTER 11

EVERYTHING WAS DIFFERENT with this pregnancy. With Taven, she felt energetic and full of life. With this baby, she had morning sickness for six months and felt fatigued most of the time. Even with pregnancy challenges, she joyfully prepared for their child's arrival.

When Bryce was born, he was lively and full of energy. He was the perfect expression of both Delaney and Beckett and was the center of attention, not just in their eyes but seemingly to the whole world. The nurses commented at the fine features, thick hair, and mature face of the newborn infant. Complete strangers asked to hold Bryce in stores. People talked directly to Bryce, forgetting others were there, including his big brother, Taven.

Delaney felt in awe of this child as he grew older because he was so mature and wise. While she had a loving, close bond with Taven, it felt a little like a buddy or pal, but with Bryce, it was like a supernatural visitor who chose to live in this body and selected her to be his mother. She was along for the ride but not entirely sure she was deserving. His eyes danced like flames, mesmerizingly flickering as he talked. He was so smart too! It was hard to stay ahead of him, and it was obvious he had his father's good looks and athletic ability. She sometimes marveled at him and wondered why God gave all His gifts to this one person. She was grateful but found it a little overwhelming because of how much she loved him.

No one had to tell her this time. She saw it early on and, while visiting with Taven's doctor, Delaney asked that they run a panel of tests just for her peace of mind. She didn't want to be the paranoid mom who worried about everything, but instinctively she knew she was a practical woman with an unofficial medical degree and the world's leading expert on this disease, having cared for Taven for eight years. It may be unlikely, as the doctor said, but it wasn't impossible.

The medical team couldn't explain how it could happen again; they just knew it did. As tests confirmed her greatest fear, she couldn't help but be amazed at the irony of it all! She had two abortions, and now God would take the two children she bore. It was the ultimate payback, and being a good mother to these two was not enough to truly right the wrong. What was she thinking? That God actually loved her! What a crock of shit. All the promises felt good while they lasted, and the way she felt in those quiet moments with her children were too good to be true and must come to an end like all good things. She needed God, but felt deep down that He has made it clear that He hates her. She shed no tears as the doctors tried to explain what they didn't understand. She had spent countless hours privately pleading with her unwanted friend, Fear, not to overcome her son but had already resolved herself to it.

There was solace in the fact that both boys had the same disease and could support one another. Delaney's identity became so wrapped up in being the mother of two sick kids that she wasn't sure who she was anymore, but there wasn't time for thinking deeply about it.

Beckett was a rock. He didn't always understand the brief episodes of hysteria that came like waves when Claire and Kinsley were around, and as much as he wanted to protect Delaney from it, he knew that they were able to express all that Delaney couldn't bear. Delaney needed them to say and do what she felt because if she did it, she would break in half and gush out like a raging river, and that would help no one, especially Taven and Bryce.

Some of the hardest times were when the boys were feeling well, playing sports, and appearing healthy. Delaney would look at them being normal, and try with her whole heart to relish the moment, but she also knew it wouldn't last. She longed to feel only one feeling at a time. She wondered what it would be like to be happy, get devastating news, be sad, or angry without the complication of having them combined. For her, emotions swirled around below the surface in a big, jumbled mess. She was hurt, elated, devastated, joyful, hopeless, and hopeful all at the same time. No one could fully understand and Delaney didn't have the ability or energy to express it.

Taven was a typical teenager but with a short future that ticked like an alarm clock set to go off at an unknown time. He loved baseball, being with friends, and girls. He lived life knowing he may not have a tomorrow. He loved fiercely and was forever Delaney's first love. She wasn't thrilled to learn of a grandchild with a girlfriend he didn't intend to marry, but she knew him better than anyone else, and having something to live on after he was gone would be his greatest desire. Later, she would treasure his little girl more than she could ever imagine possible.

After a liver transplant, he, like any teenager, occasionally drank alcohol which caused cirrhosis of the new liver, and even though she pleaded with the hospital to put him on the transplant list again, they refused, inciting a death sentence in her eyes. She wanted to be angry. She wanted to hate them, curse them, and forever damn them each personally, but she didn't have it in her because Taven wasn't that way. He loved, got knocked down, then kept on loving. He understood the ramifications of his actions, and Delaney knew Bryce was watching everyone in preparation for his time to face life and death decisions.

Taven met the love of his life only a few short years before his death. Kristen was the only woman for him and the only person who could measure up to the other woman in his life, his mother. Taven and Kristen were so much alike; it was uncanny. Only a woman as strong as Kristin could survive such fierce love with a foretold ending. It was inspiring to watch Taven and Kristen's life together unfold, and Delaney felt a renewed hope in God because only He could have orchestrated this perfect ending to Taven's story. Delaney was grateful to share the spotlight with Kristen as Taven lay in the hospital room. They were both so lucky to call him "theirs."

While the world carried on, their world stopped, and although people stepped in and out for a few moments at a time, it was their life all the time. They could see that as their visitors entered the elevator to head home, they squeezed their loved ones a little tighter, dialed frantically to hear their voices, or dove deep into their own thoughts, trying to make sense of it all. Delaney had seen it a million times. They were grateful not to be on her train and desperate to jump back to their own, but Delaney knew nothing other than this, and her wisdom, so painfully obtained, would be a guiding force for her young daughter-in-law.

CHAPTER 12

W HEN THE TIME CAME, Taven moved beyond Delaney's reach and into a new world. She felt hollow and lost as if she had been the one to escape. All she wanted was to crumble under the weight of sadness and the cruelty of the clock that continued to move forward. She couldn't acknowledge her shredded soul because staring back at her was her thirteen-year-old son with understanding eyes that drew her in, so full of wisdom. Bryce's future was always tethered to Taven's. Not many of us can understand another human's walk like they did because they were living it together.

Bryce's outlook was uniquely his own from the time of being a little boy. He seemed more mature than others as he played rambunctiously and with all the zest of the others but was always acutely aware of dangers lurking insidiously about that no one else ever noticed. He cherished every day, and the ones where he felt strong and "normal" were even more precious. Bryce had the ability at a young age to value life. He seemed to understand and value a friend's presence, health, and opportunities bigger than his own. Even now, after Taven's passing, Bryce seemingly picked himself back up and carried on saying, "Live life as if nothing ever happened."

Following Bryce's lead, Beckett and Delaney honored their son, Taven with dignity and hope. James was heartbroken but had prepared himself over many years to accept it as any other unavoidable life event. Like Delaney, he had moved on to remarry and have more children. Delaney and James shared some beautiful yet tragic years together. She was grateful for him because he helped her heal to the point she could enter into a relationship with someone like Beckett.

Bryce was becoming his own man. He was able to process life and death in light of his own calculated future. Delaney couldn't grieve for Taven because it would steal her precious time with Bryce. She had stuffed so many things down into that inner layer and discovered there was room in the abyss for more. With a smile and brave exterior, Delaney stopped time by holding her breath and taking a mental snapshot to be sure she had memories. She understood death's finality more now than ever and vowed to make the most of every day with Bryce and Beckett.

Bryce demanded much from his life. He pressed into the joyful times as well as the sad ones. Athletic, funny, handsome, spiritual, smart, and kind-hearted were words used to describe him, and as a high schooler, he was loved by classmates, teachers, and members of the small town where he had grown up. Bryce dedicated his days to making others feel seen, valued, and heard. There was some celebrity status he enjoyed because he impacted anyone who ever met him, and celebrities and sports icons were no exception. Even the famous left the hospital, unable to shake the desire to be in Bryce's presence rather than the other way around. Musicians followed his social media, baseball players dedicated games, and friends flocked to be with him, whether at the hospital or home. Delaney experienced a new high in being "Bryce's Mom." She and Beckett knew it as an honor and treasured every reference to their identity in him.

Just as the planets rotate around the sun, Bryce became the center of the universe for thousands of people united in prayer and hoping for his healing. It didn't seem possible that God would dare take someone so wonderful and full of His light away from this world, but on September 13, 2014, Bryce died, and it was a catastrophic blow to their souls. The ties that bound them, the coupler of hearts—so sturdy and forged of iron gained through tears and hope, came unbound and what remained seemed out of control, chaotic, and lost as the world moved on. The "Save Bryce" campaign, the prayer meetings, the laying on of hands, the fundraisers, the waiting room full of visitors, the doctor's best efforts, the dedicated websites, and a young man's faith wasn't enough to keep him here.

Delaney walked in a fog for several weeks, and Beckett busied himself with a project on family land. He needed his roots and something to live for. Delaney relied on the strength of others to do the simplest of daily tasks. She lacked the motivation and stamina to keep walking through the inevitable waves of grief that came crashing in. To the amazement of others, she did it, though. She got up, got dressed, and continued to live life outside her home. In some ways, it was easier to be out and about than to have all the reminders of her precious boys that filled her home. She fought to stay connected to Beckett and let him lead them through the darkest days of her life. So much had been stolen from her, but this marriage would not be another casualty. It was all she had, and she once again purposed her heart to stay alive with Beckett because that is what her boys would want.

CHAPTER 13

DEATH, THE FAMILIAR FRIEND, had visited once more. "Stolen Lives" was a mysterious phrase that Delaney found perplexing, forbidding, and thought-provoking, but now it held no mystery at all. She was well acquainted with its curse and believed its insidious roots were a message straight from God those many years ago that her life was too happy and He would put into action His plan to ensure the lives that mattered the most to her would be stolen from her one person at a time. His plan was so much worse than simply taking her father's life on that birthday morning. She knew that He would pluck everything from her slowly, painfully until she had nothing left. As bad as she wanted to die, she knew He would grant her a very long life of suffering just to demonstrate the depth of his cruelty. After all, she deserved it. She had taken the lives of two babies, and now it was payback time. She paid her debt, but the interest was yet to be paid, which she rationalized must be lived out before she could join her boys in the beyond.

Life without the boys was dull, and Delaney wanted so badly to ignore the tremendous impact her kids had on this world because every compliment was balanced with a stabbing pain somewhere further inside than she knew existed. She was too much the center of attention. Why couldn't everyone just leave them alone? What must she do to become invisible? Delaney knew instinctively that she would never be invisible, especially to her boys. There were moments in the night's quiet still where she felt their presence.

One afternoon, she gathered up her courage and visited the boys' graves. She gravitated to the cemetery when life got hectic, and she needed a connection back to them. Being alone there didn't feel the same as being alone at home and she wondered why. One afternoon, Delaney felt especially burdened by the reality that they weren't there, and everything seemed dim and dreary. The clouds were low to the ground like they were closing in on her. The grass was dry and brittle under her feet and difficult to walk on in her flip flops. She sat on a bench nearby and let herself cry. It was an indulgence she rarely afforded herself and it scared her not knowing if she would recover once the tears flowed. Off in the distance, she saw two delicate, white butterflies flitting between a tombstone and a bush. It caught her attention and she looked for more but saw only the two. As she watched them, they came towards her as if playing chase with one another. They danced all around her for several minutes. Delaney giggled and truly enjoyed their shenanigans. She was grateful for their presence and thanked God for sending them. Her boys were with her in this moment and for the first time in a very long time, she was at peace.

Butterflies would continue to appear out of nowhere, and she often thought she received other messages from beyond. She could never tell anyone about it because they would think she was crazy, but she felt in communication with the boys through them. There just seemed to be a "knowing" between them, and when she wanted to stay in bed with the covers over her head, she would feel their prodding and encouragement, and she reluctantly obeyed. People marveled at her strength and would comment about how well she was doing. She would laugh inside and joke with Taven and Bryce that if they only knew, she was barely pulling it together. It seemed to be a little joke the three had with each other. She liked being in communion with their spirits. She didn't know where God was in all this, but as long as she had peace from her boys, she would be okay.

Beckett loved and admired Delaney, and she felt the same way about him. Given different circumstances, their lives would be absolutely perfect. Their happiness gauge was a hundred percent with a grief limit on it, dampening it to a sixty percent max. There was a ceiling on joy, and they stayed right at that ceiling, giving it their all, hoping that when they died, they would experience the fullness of the highs because they had endured such lows. Busyness was a friend, and if they didn't sit still, they could manage. Days came and went with the rising and setting of the sun. The systematic advancement of time marched on, and they both wondered what would lie before them that would feel any different than today.

Instinctively, Delaney knew God would take Beckett first. It seemed like a fitting end to be all alone here on this earth while praying constantly to be spared another day. On a beautiful autumn day, Beckett drew his last breath. He had been sick for a while and Delaney came to peace with letting him go. She whispered into his ear that she would be okay and encouraged him to go on to the other side to be reunited with Taven and Bryce. She knew he understood as his lips curved upward into a slight smile and his eyelids relaxed. His breathing wasn't labored, and peace filled the room. She knew that releasing him from this life was the right thing to do but didn't want to acknowledge the consequences just yet.

Of all the intimate moments they shared together, this was by far the most profound. Her spirit had been woven together with his so many years ago and she could feel each stich being ripped out in order to salvage her ragged self that was left. She was surprised at the feeling death had over her once again. Even with practice, the breaking of the heart and ripping away of a soul was like an anchor down deep dragging the bottom because of a fierce storm above water. She was somewhere in between. Again, knowing the right thing to do, she kissed his lips, stroked his hair, and lovingly thanked him for being her life. Beckett's chest simply rested as another breath was no longer needed. It was over and like a channel on her old childhood television, her mind switched to black and white static as there was no longer any programming. She rested her head on his chest and softly cried. The room filled with medical professionals but none of it mattered. She had lost the last person she loved.

After a long while, Delaney noticed how people looked at her. It was as if she was a frail, pathetic old woman incapable of understanding what had just happened. She was so tired and couldn't exert the energy it would require convincing them she knew more than most about life, death, tragedy, blessings, and curses. The devil had been a constant companion while she hoped for a cosmic alternative. Her faith in God had grown over the years because she was so well acquainted with the alternative. God was her punching bag, and she knew He could take it, but now she had no fight left in her. While packing her belongings, she resigned herself to outliving everyone with as much grace as she could muster. Her bitterness had been a constant companion, but Beckett had a way of forcing it into the background. She would honor his memory by living another day as if nothing ever happened.

CHAPTER 14

Y ou have seen so much on this journey that it just doesn't feel
right to have a vantage point to see someone's pain so clearly. It's
difficult to witness, and even though you want to look away, you crave
more. It is the shared human experience that draws you in. You wonder
what will happen next. When will Delaney's luck turn? Why did all
these events need to happen? It feels unjust, and even though you trust
that a positive outcome will be had, you find yourself bristling inside,
and that tension needs an outlet. You think back on that beautiful
train station where the journey started and trust the purpose of it all
was worth the pain of the human experience.

Your questions are multiplying instead of subsiding. Then, your spirit
awakens with the sense someone is coming alongside you, possibly with
answers. You look anxiously around, but no one is there, yet peace
is flowing to you. You are on Delaney's train and see other eternals
moving above, below, and around you at lightning speeds. They are
connected to Delaney's journey and you marvel at the amount of activity happening around this segment. It is as if reinforcements have been
tripled and you don't want to miss anything.

Peace is the most precious gift of heaven. It wraps you up with a
secure familiarity like your grandmother's tattered, well-loved, favorite
quilt. Your breathing slows to a natural and consistent pattern. Each
measured with doses of love and understanding beyond the present in
cadence with that which is ancient and holds the future.

He is here now deep within you, on the shallows around you, and
within every particle of your being. You feel Jesus's hand gently cup your
shoulder. When He touches you, love radiates through your body. As

you turn towards Him, His eyes are full of fiery color. You are transported inside His being. A place to rest has been provided before you
thought to ask. Your spirit literally rests in His. His breath becomes
fused with yours, and as your mind relaxes, your spirit hears Him ask,
"Who do you say that I am?"

As a reflection, you answer, "God and the Son of God." For a brief
second, you wonder if you are right, then realize there could be no
other answer.

His cells smile, and yours are grateful to return the sentiment. Jesus
then whispers, "Would God forsake those He loves?"

From a pure place inside you, you answer, "No, never."

He responds, "There is much to Delaney's story that you have not
seen but you know enough that compassion and understanding have
taken residence in your heart for her journey. It is her race but now
you are invested in seeing her finish with dignity and grace. Travel
with her as she discovers all that has been orchestrated for her good.
Delight in knowing Me and seeing the victory that has come from all
things, even the pain." Trusting Him is so easy when you are with Him
and you now feel renewed to finish the race with her.

As you look back towards the scene, time has advanced, and Delaney
is a much old woman lying in a hospital bed. She has grown weary and
wears the daily struggle as an oversized coat concealing her strength
and fortitude that has been developed in recent years. It is at this
moment; that you remember seeing her in your mind's eye—the old
woman in the park with a walker. She was talking with Jesus but not
knowing it. She had recalled the day so long ago that her spirit died,
and now, you are witnessing her body struggling for life.

Alone in her room, Delaney is thankful for the quiet night shift.
With the boys, she always appreciated the stillness of the night shift.
Flowers filled the room, and their fragrance was amplified so she could
appreciate the variety of sentiment behind each one and those who sent
them. Her years without Beckett were unexpectedly fruitful. She did as
she promised and stayed connected to a network of friends and found

new depths of forgiveness and contentment with her circumstances. She had come to a place where lessons learned were helpful to younger women just starting out which gave her pleasure.

Every breath is shallow, and you find yourself matching yours to her cadence. Your spirit is now so closely tied to hers that you feel inclined to crawl into her bed and cradle her small, frail body with your spirit. You are grateful for the opportunity to comfort her and Delaney responds by resting even deeper with each blissful breath. You know time is still moving forward but it feels as if the minutes expanded to allow for supernatural, experiential time.

Delaney is ready to gently release her spirit from the confines of this world. You notice the wall clock shows 4:15 PM. A deep sense of purpose and appropriateness fills the room, and your trust in God is further confirmed, knowing all things have meaning. As if she had been here before, Delaney calmy and confidently rises in her spirit out of her earthly body. With fully renewed energy, she walks towards the gentle warm light that has presented itself and filled the room. You follow her with pure curiosity, not because you don't know what is next, but because you wonder how Delaney will receive the world that is your home.

Delaney puts her outstretched hand into another's. She moves closer, closes her eyes and rests her head on their chest while caring arms surround her with the kindest embrace. Bryce also closes his eyes and relishes this moment. The woman for whom he admires above all others has arrived. Even though they have never been apart, it is this moment that all of heaven has been waiting for; it is now complete. Delaney pulls back to see her son's face. With every tear that trickles down her face, time is reversed, and her youth is restored to a younger, vibrant self. Without interrupting their embrace, they are transported out of time without knowing anything beyond their love and tremendous bond. Delaney says nothing aloud, but you know there is much being communicated between mother and son floating in a sea of love for one another.

Delaney holds her son's face with both hands to get a good look into his eyes just as he smiles with the excitement of her arrival. As she turns to look around, we have arrived at a beautiful farm with sun-kissed green pastures swaying to a gentle breeze. Delaney sees you, and you prepare to introduce yourself, but she immediately hugs you, caresses your face, and says, "Thank you, my friend, for being there with me and being with me now." You are surprised that you been included in this moment and seems to know you already.

Before you can say anything, Delaney turns back to Bryce and asks, "Where is He?" There is a twinkle of anticipation in her eyes and a bounce in her step.

Bryce chuckles, answering, "I knew you would ask for Him first thing. I've heard some of your lively conversations over the years filled with life's biggest questions, but first, some people want to see you."

As he said this, music floats into your awareness, and you notice it coming from a barn surrounded by a massive wildflower patch. A truly genuine smile comes over Delaney like you have not seen before. A brilliant, flowing, holographic spirit jumps from within Delaney with her realization that her precious father, Dennis, is in that barn playing his guitar like he did every night in the small house by the tracks. Her love leaps, and a treasure chest of hope is unlocked, knowing a reunion with him is awaiting her. She takes your hand and wraps her arm around Bryce's waist, and off you go towards the joyous sound beckoning her arrival.

You are filled with questions popping away inside your mind like tiny exciting, multi-colored firecrackers; but, at the same time, you have complete peace that all is as it should be and the need for understanding is so far beyond you that you choose to simply bathe in the honor of being in this moment.

CHAPTER 15

The journey to the barn was a floating sensation, but rather than being released from gravity, you move along an invisible cellular current. The ability to smell the grass is more like a conversation than an observation. The music from the barn is moving its way to you and ushering you on a path of elated emotion, waking up every blade of grass, blooming flower, and living thing. The butterflies were amazing, and Delaney cherished each and every one because, over the years, butterflies had a personal meaning of encouragement from the other side. They were the perfect escort!

As Delaney walks towards the barn, a lone fiddler leaves the doorway and meets her steps until Dennis is serenading his sweet daughter, with whom he has delighted in. The song is unlike anything Delaney has ever heard and yet so familiar she is able to take it deep into her soul for safekeeping. It is the song of her life filled with love, laughter, disbelief, sorrow, regret, and disdain, but, in this place, she is able to absorb it all and acknowledge it as an achievement, and the title of it washes over her like a sweet melodic hope. "Well Done" would become her anthem, and anyone who would meet her would instantly understand her struggles, losses, redemption, and impact as written from Dennis' heavenly perspective. It is only from here that Dennis could have written such a masterpiece; it is only from the safety of this place that she would allow herself to take it all in.

His instrument was magnificent, but she was focused on his eyes. Her father's eyes were captivating and held within them every vision he had for her, every prayer he prayed, every dream redeemed, every consolation in her deepest despair. He is standing before her, celebrating her life just as he had always done, and although she worked so hard to hide from him, she was intensely grateful that he had seen it all. They were never really separated, and although she didn't understand it fully, it was easy to accept. This is a homecoming but also an acknowledgment of the unbreakable, eternal connection that has always been there.

Over Dennis' shoulder, Delaney catches a glimpse of Kinsley and Momma. They are the most beautiful women she had ever known. She is keenly aware they all favor one another. There were other women with them. She could tell that they were also "Cut from the same cloth," as her mother always said. Each woman was incredibly courageous with anthems of their own, and their stories were linked by decades and situations that defined them and cut them into beautiful, picturesque beings proud of their accumulated wisdom.

She investigated each face knowing them intimately, not as in a first meeting, but as close confidants. Each woman hugged her with their eyes, and there was an appreciative acknowledgment deep down in her soul unlike anything she had ever known. A deep sense of gratitude filled Delaney as she understood that their lives were woven together with a great and perfect purpose.

Like a rush of adrenaline, she understood it all in complete fullness, then it receded away to only the part she could comprehend. Unlike her life before, she was at complete peace knowing that what she understood was all that she needed to understand, and when she needed more, God would give it to her. These women were her lineage. Those before her and all those after her sharing in a tapestry of time perfectly coordinated to accomplish a complex pattern of life designed perfectly for a desperate world.

Sweetness floated past her in a soft scent that told her heart that her sweet son, Taven, was there. She shifted her glance ever so slightly to see his gaze upon her. Her heart melted, and their special connection was inconceivably more intense and powerful. Taven was her firstborn. He was a magnificent gift that, at the time, she didn't think she deserved, and yet, in this moment, Delaney realizes Taven was the perfect gift from heaven that God gave to heal her broken heart, and she was Taven's eternal reward.

Taven realized his mother was honored among all mothers. She was revered in the eternal community by the she loved her children and earned her significance through perseverance. He was so proud to be her son. Now, standing outside time, Delaney could see that they lived each for the other.

She hugged him as if they had never been separated, and a portion of her wondered if they ever really had. She couldn't remember a time without him, but her brain knew there had been years on earth where she lamented his absence. As with the women, she was at peace knowing but not knowing the details and trusted she would learn more about it later.

Suddenly, Delaney is reminded of the beautiful scent that floated into her car many years ago in the hospital parking garage with Taven. It was diagnosis day, and that smell was exactly the same as what is surrounding her now. Taven immediately recognizes her curiosity and says, "Yes, Mom. It's the same smell. The presence of heaven was with us that day." Delaney is astonished at the realization that heaven was interacting with them on the earth. By allowing her and Taven to get a whiff of heaven on that dark day, God was reminding Delaney of her true home and the trust that overflows here.

The barn was so beautifully decorated. Light illuminated everything and everyone. She looked around, there were mementos from her life assimilated together. Gucci, her little dog, pictures, and artwork from the boys caught her eye. Old trunks lined the outskirts of what seemed to be a giant dancefloor. The decorative rhinestone saddle that she always loved from her sister's barn hung overhead and illuminated the walls with droplets of light, creating a festive mood. Each old trunk was different in size and style and had quilts and blankets covering them. Sitting on top of each trunk was a person looking like the trunk's owner. Some had pens and paper, and others had fancy quills and scrolls.

Delaney was fascinated with the trunk guardians. Bryce explained that every word, thought, deed had been documented for Abba Father. Angels were assigned the important task of watching over and to care for the precious, commemorative cargo. Her life was held in these trunks for safekeeping. Every tear that was shed, every joyous burst of laughter, and every pleading prayer had been observed, documented, and communicated for her review. She was in awe of the meticulous details of the task. She hadn't thought that these things would matter after she died but has come to understand she was very wrong.

In fact, these angels have been assigned to her from the moment a train left the station to capture it all as a treasure she would spend eternity contemplating and learning of His greatness towards her. Nothing intimidated her. She knew there would be moments that were shameful in time, but here, there was no fear, and her place was secure, and she felt highly valued. Her teachers would share it with her, and she couldn't wait to begin.

One question bubbled to the surface of her consciousness. As she turned to ask, Bryce answered before she uttered a word. Bryce said, "You want to know why Taven and I had to die as we did and why God hated you so much that he took us despite your cries for help. I don't think you can comprehend the answer without experiencing it for yourself. Would you like me to take you to the answers?" Delaney's heart leaped with the satisfaction that her words were really heard, and her heartache was known. For so long, she thought she was invisible to God. She closed her eyes for a moment to take in the depth of love she felt surrounding her. Courage filled her to accept the answers about to be revealed.

Beckett stepped up to reassure Delaney that the journey was worth it, and he would be here when she returns. She collected her thoughts and resolved herself to doing whatever it took to finally get answers to her deepest questions. She was grateful for Beckett's reassurance and thanked him for his steadfast love. As she refocused on Bryce, she looked past his eyes and into his soul. She could see color beams of electricity racing all around. Together they were transported into a swirling spectacle of light bouncing through them in beautiful harmony with their spirits.

A network of illuminated trains on shiny golden tracks raced all around Delaney and Taven. Their focus was directed on one railcar with an expansive stained-glass roof and cedar siding. An infinity butterfly symbol was artistically constructed with expert craftmanship. The array of colors and intricate design were unlike anything she had ever seen, and it literally took her breath away. Delaney was thrilled as Bryce set course for that car. As they approached, the rough cedar exterior became transparent, and they gently floated in with ease.

CHAPTER 16

As soon as Delaney sees the dusty field next to the curve of the train tracks, she quickly turns to Bryce, pleading, "Not here, not now, there isn't a need to be here." Bryce didn't say a word but looked lovingly into her eyes, and she was immediately calm as peace washed over her.

She breathed in his confidence, and then he said to her, "Mom, this is a very important moment in history. You were thought of before the foundation of time, and it was in this moment that the world recognized your greatness. The world didn't like your power."

Delaney was confused. If anything, she had lived her life feeling powerless. *What is he talking about?* she thought. What was the alternative to being in this moment? Being dead was still new to her, and other than being with Bryce, there was nothing else that she could think to do. This felt like a divine appointment, and something Bryce had been assigned to do and important to him. He seemed so prepared and had a mission that was somehow associated with her healing.

She wondered how she could still feel reluctant in heaven. What about the "No tears" and "No care in the world" that she had always been taught about heaven? Her mind snapped to the word *trust*, and she had an ah-ha moment where she thought, *This is what trust should feel like. I may be reluctant, but fear is absent. I'm willing to move forward because I trust him. Wow! This is different.* As Bryce patiently waited, it was as if he could see the wheels turning in her mind, and he gave her enough time to work it out. Her reluctance turned to a glimmer of hope. She still wasn't sure, but she trusted love would motivate this moment.

The train whistle could be heard off in the distance, and from a bird's eye view, Delaney watched as she, Kinsley, and Pappa came spilling out the front door of their tiny little house. They were a loud bunch, and their happiness filled her heart. As they raced toward the tracks, Delaney noticed someone else. *Where did he come from?* she thought. He was a tall, handsome man about the same age as her father, running up to greet the girls. As they approached, he turned to run with them, laughing and enjoying the moment as much as her father.

Having not thought of it for a lifetime, Delaney remembered the essence of the conversation she was having with her father. It was about her "Arriving on time," "Needed by the world," and "Carrying something special into the world." She had long ago decided that they were childish lies to be buried down deep, but, now, she recognized it as absolute truth, and the Originator of this legacy was with her father, delighting as wisdom was being passed down and revealed to ones so young.

As the group got nearer to the tracks, the train made its way forward. The tracks illuminated with excitement, and rays of color bounced around in vibrant shades of orange, yellow, and bright pink. As the train begins to pass and their group yells out "1... 2... 3...," the magical lights dance around them and spike upwards towards the sky with each celebrated number. Delaney is mesmerized by the brilliance of it. How did she miss the light's intensity, and who was this other person?

As the tenth car begins to approach, the lights turn to blue and purple tones. The light circles around their feet, and then as the 12th car approaches, the light expands to create a box around them, hemming them in on all sides. The man turns his back to the car and stands in front of the group. Delaney sees her younger self mesmerized and fixated on the graffiti, and she feels so sad for the young girl and wants to enter the scene to cover her eyes preventing this sweet girl from seeing such a haunting sight.

The unknown man's expression turns from bright laughter to sheer determination and resolve. She was startled by the man's steely gaze of confidently restrained power. His decision to stand was a calculated action, not passive, but Delaney wasn't quite sure what it all meant. Her father's expression went from fear to resolve in an instant. The man's countenance influenced her father and his posture and expression changed. Witnessing this man's power to command light and strengthen her father suddenly helps Delaney recognize the man. It is Jesus!

Jesus and Dennis met gazes, and together they distracted the girls away from the menacing train cars. Jesus put his arm around her father, and her father smiled slightly and nodded. She isn't sure if Dennis is seeing Jesus in the natural, but she is sure he understands what Jesus is saying to him. Kinsley was still full of joy, and the light at her feet remained yellow and orange, but the rest of them had swirls of blue and purple around them. As the graffiti's car passed out of sight, Delaney noticed herself and Jesus glancing back at it, understanding its significance.

Jesus knelt next to little girl Delaney, lifted her chin, and breathed into her ear. He was positioning her for courage and infusing her with the power to push through. The girl pulled her shoulders back and shook out her arms like shaking off the dust. As they walked the tracks back the house, Jesus walked with the girls and enjoyed the feel of the tracks underfoot. He felt proud of His girls and knew the enemy had seen their great worth. His plans for them would not be thwarted.

Bryce turned to Delaney and said, "This was the moment everything changed for you, wasn't it?" Delaney, with tears resting on the ridge of her heart, nodded yes. Bryce continued, "When I first arrived in eternity, Jesus met me and brought me to this moment. He explained that this little girl would one day become my mother.

He infused you with the His courage to help you endure this life. He chose you from before the foundation of the world to be my mother, and that would come with incredible joy and devastating pain, but you were the only person in history up for the task." Bryce also explained, "The world has an enemy, and the enemy stands outside time and knows who the 'Triumphant ones' will be. The message on the train was just that. It was a message from the other side meant to scare you as a little girl and create a wound that could be agitated many times over. Wisdom is a threat to the evil one."

Delaney took it all in. She mused to herself out loud, "So that is Jesus. Why didn't I see Him or that day? Why didn't I feel His presence or the lights? If I was so important, why wouldn't He have just destroyed the train car before I saw it or eliminate the one who sent the hideous message?" Without feeling anger or bitterness, Delaney was simply perplexed and asked Bryce the questions of her heart. She knew the answers would come when she was ready for understanding.

Bryce lifted her chin, just as Jesus had for that little girl; he blew sweetly into her ear, and even though he knew it wasn't infused with the same power and might as had been with Jesus, he recreated the moment and then whispered, "All that you seek will be given unto you." Now, Delaney felt like the child, and her wise son, who has spent more time here, become the teacher. Together, they will discover great meanings in life.

She felt so grateful for this moment with him. They watched the family enjoy breakfast together and were warmed by the simplicity of their life filled with love. Slowly, the walls of their tiny home became transparent, and angels, thousands and thousands of angels appeared. They, too, were witnessing this moment. The angels understood the significance, which made Delaney feel as though she only understood a small portion of its meaning. Time seemed to stand still as they observed the family enjoying one another, but Delaney, having lived it, knew it hadn't.

Standing in the simple kitchen, lost in the moment, the wooden floor suddenly begins to split apart plank by plank, revealing the most beautiful blue, cloud-filled sky below them. Their current surroundings dissolve, and Taven casually approaches Delaney and Bryce. The boys exchange a familiar handshake, and Taven sweetly hugs his mother. Taven whispers in Delaney's ear, "I've been waiting to share a moment with you." Delaney's eyes light up as her mind sifts through the possibilities of what her next adventure will be. She dreamed of this for so long, and now the moment is here. She can hug her boys, celebrate the men before her, and catch that ever-present twinkle in their big, beautiful eyes. As soon as she contemplates sitting on a cloud or flying through the universe with them, she sees a more serious intention in Taven's expression and resets her mind for another train car visit.

CHAPTER 17

As she descends into the next car, an ominous smoke surrounds it, tinged with dark grey, blue, and purple tones. The colors represented by the smoke aren't beautiful like the colors of light she had seen on the previous visit. It was a mucky, dirty smoke with a foul stench. As they moved through it, Delaney was surprised that she was no longer offended by the odor or feel any residue. It was as if they had slid down an invisible tube so as not to be bothered by such things. As they entered this point in time, Delaney knew instantly where she was and shivered at the idea of this memory. The dirty smoke was hovering over the railyard, seeping out into the streets of her precious hometown. Delaney wanted to exhale a huge wind to clear the area and rid the place of it. Her disdain for its presence was palpable.

Bryce observed her bristling at its sight and gently took her hand into his. She looked into his eyes and forced a smile, but she wasn't ready yet to release her uneasiness. It had been a comfort to her for many years, and her hatred of whatever was present was her badge of "Kinkaid Family Honor." Her hatred of evil's presence was a demonstration of her love. She often felt like she was the only one who could see it. Wasn't it her duty to be aware and hate it? How could she let that go?

Delaney sees sweet Mr. Joe pacing back and forth. He is waiting for her to run through the gates of the railyard after school. He desperately wants to intercept her and prevent her from the trauma he himself was experiencing as his best friend struggles. He wipes the sweat off his brow and somehow commands time to slow down because he needs to find Delaney in the crowd of people, the chaos in front of him. His whispered mantra is amplified so she can hear him repeating, "Please God, Please God," as he scans the scene. Time is a kind friend to him, and she watches how his brain is able to process each face rushing by, the people in each vehicle, and the smallest details of the moment. She sees his eyes lock in on the little girl standing in wonder outside the gate.

Joe sees young Delaney's questioning mind and watches her reroute to west boundary. He knows she is looking for the loose chain-link panel. Joe anticipates her path and intercepts her running towards the accident. With a quick, "Thank God," he swoops her into his arms and tries to prevent her from going any further. She relaxes a bit, and it seems as though he has been successful, but then a cry is heard, and he knows every cell in her body is linked to it. She is prewired to hear her father's voice. She wiggles to break loose in an instant and runs towards the crowd.

Delaney locks eyes with Mr. Joe as he panics, having let loose of young Delaney. She understands that he is trying to spare her from the traumatic images of her father that she will carry with her for the rest of her life. As her little self runs into the crowd, she sees the menacing greyish-green smoke hovering inches over the ground, polluting the atmosphere. Delaney wishes she hadn't held a grudge against Mr. Joe. He was only trying to help, but her little girl self saw it as a betrayal of their friendship.

Mr. Cathaway steps up to speak to the little girl. The depth of his sorrow is so significant that Delaney feels sorry for him. This day would cause a wound in him that he would bear for the rest of his life. As he bends down to talk to the girl, a huge warrior-like angel comes near to ensure the girl can focus, and Mr. Cathaway has the freedom to think and speak directly to the little girl with a calm voice. He had Delaney's attention for a time allowing her little mind to catch up. Delaney looks on this scene remembering the calm exchange between she and Mr. Cathaway. She couldn't have known an angel was protecting them.

As Delaney dreads the unfolding scene, heavenly Dennis comes up beside her and puts his arms around her. Not realizing she had stopped breathing, Delaney let out a deep sigh of relief, remembering that her healed, happy father was standing next to her, and the end of the story is one of love and restoration. He gave Delaney a nod of courage, and her hesitation subsided.

Delaney turns to her father and buries her face into his chest. He is strong and warm like always, but she could also feel something else. It was as if she could feel his transparency. His whole soul was known to her whole soul. He hugged her tight and, without saying a word, encouraged her to continue viewing the past. Courage filled her from the top down, and without fully comprehending it, her mind converted from dread and fear to anticipation of the healing she knew was now arriving.

The little girl's gut-wrenching sobs being poured out over her father's body were somehow transforming in Delaney's hearing. She knew the cries were ones of pain, but there was also a melodic overtone similar to chimes or glass bells ringing that she didn't remember hearing. She noticed little sparks of light twinkling like fireflies all-round the crowd. As the sparkles moved around, the green smoke scattered until finally, it had been pushed completely out of sight from the scene. Heaven was present and intervening to shift the atmosphere. Her cries transformed into a melody and the menacing smoke was cleared with Heaven's help.

Dennis squeezed Delaney's shoulders a little tighter and whispered, "Now, watch this." The little lights moved and danced like a beautiful, coordinated swarm around and through the people. As they enveloped Dennis' body, Delaney could see his soul rising up out of his broken body and standing tall. The lights illuminated him, and his eyes met Delaney's. *Can he see me?* she thought. The healed Dennis took an intentional step in her direction as if to answer her question. He walked up to her and embraced her while her heavenly host, Dennis, remained hugging her from behind. She was now encapsulated in two versions of her father. *How could this be?* she thought, but the desire to keep thinking melted away, and deep peace to just rest in this moment took over. She rested in his arms and let love restore her.

Delaney had intimate knowledge of the rest of the story. She had pledged to blame someone for Dennis' death. In fact, it wasn't just one person but most people through her life. She grieved the day her father was taken but seeing it from this perspective had changed everything. It was the root of so many wounds that would stay with her the rest of her life. She didn't need to see anymore of the rail-yard experience. The healing ointment that was applied knowing her father was okay erased all the other hurts compounded over the years.

Bryce knew the oaths taken that day such as "my life doesn't matter" and "I have to fend for myself" were defense mechanisms that are no longer needed. Bryce handed Delaney an ornate, gold bracelet and said, "This was given to me by Jesus to give to you while on this journey. He wants you to know how much you matter to Him." Before Bryce finished the sentence, a beautiful ruby stone sprouted up in the setting. She knew it signified love and acceptance even in the midst of great misunderstanding.

You have been here before. In fact, it was one of the first scene you visited fresh from the station. Jesus had comforted Delaney's father as he stepped out of his body. Dennis spoke with Abba and came to an agreement. Then, he encouraged and strengthened Mrs. Hughes before walking out of time and into eternity with Abba. The love between a father and child is one of the greatest testimonies that ever existed. It makes you appreciate how thin the veil is between heaven and earth and the sacrifice Abba made by sending His Son into time.

CHAPTER 18

Without a way of knowing how long it had been, Delaney felt the need to slowly leave her father's warm, familiar embrace and rejoin the journey she was now experiencing. Her father's presence just simply and slowly faded away while Taven appeared. *Oh, those eyes!* she thought. Taven's eyes were mesmerizing, and for so long on earth, all she ever wanted was to gaze at them again. Now, it was happening, and there wasn't any rush or awkwardness. She felt like she could look into his face and soul for as long as she desired, and it would be exactly what she should be doing. Her smile broke the moment. It delighted Taven so much to see her happy. He had never known her without that tiny veil of distrust from years of believing happiness was not hers to possess. Now, his greatest prayer for her had been answered. She was truly happy and without any fear of losing the feeling.

Delaney's gaze continued as if in a trance. On earth, she gazed into his daughter's eyes over the years, seeing Taven through her. It gave Delaney comfort, and she cherished the fact that Jayden had inherited those beautiful eyes. But now, Delaney's mind was so sharp that it held a perfect memory of Jayden's eyes, and she heard the Holy Spirit whisper to her that they were indeed the very same.

"But I thought everyone's eyes were completely unique to them?" she replied.

Holy Spirit answered, "Indeed they are, but for you, God wanted you not to miss a moment's connection with Taven, so he made an exception for Jayden. They are indeed the exact same."

As the realization sunk in, a small white butterfly playfully dances around her and Taven. "Oh, like butterflies! They were a sign too!" Her heart leaped with overwhelming joy as she realized the intentionality behind God's existence. He designed so much for her to grasp and hold on to. It was her sustenance and the way she survived so many years. Taven giggled with joy as he watched her take in each wave of understanding. He had been watching all along as she walked through her years in time with the great satisfaction of how Abba, Jesus, and Holy Spirit worked together to cushion the blows, breathe life, and add delight where there was great sorrow. He was honored to be intertwined into these complex, magnificent relationships created so very long ago.

Delaney felt honored. A trusted friend had told her many times that she was a "Woman among women." That phrase seemed laughable and utterly untrue, but her friend believed it with her whole heart. Delaney let the phrase soak in because God Himself was demonstrating her importance in the role of time. The lives that were affected by her presence and the intricately detailed interactions of love from God that had played out over the years were becoming fully realized.

Taven felt a great deal of love and admiration for his mother, Delaney. He had already visited some of her toughest moments, and his appreciation for her went so deep that he cherished the knowledge and honorably carried it inside himself. It was time to revisit with Delaney another milestone. Delaney yielded to his lead and wanted to go where he would take her. She spotted the clouds moving beneath her, revealing the expansive train system below. She spotted a train car off in the distance and knew it was hers. It was illuminated and became a brighter and brighter beacon of light calling them as they got closer.

As she stepped inside, it was the waiting room of the clinic she had pushed out of her mind so many years ago. She knew it immediately by the smell. *We're here. This is all real. We are really here,* Delaney says to herself with a tinge of apprehension. The smell was indescribable, full of death and shame. This time, she can actually see the smell. It was a heavy fog tinted with a disgusting yellow-green that seeped out of each person, the furniture, the ceiling and the floor.

Taven explained that the people did not smell and were not "bad," but their actions carried the smell of God's enemy with them. The intention behind their actions was meant to cause her wounds for a lifetime, and because of it, God was displeased and promised to avenge the harm being done to her. Delaney cried and covered her eyes. The compassion she felt for the doctor and nurses was overwhelming. How could they have known all that was happening around them? The complete picture is so much greater than the tiny view they had. If only she had known to trust in the "larger view," how different her life would have been.

She couldn't bear to witness what she had done; then, Jesus stepped into the room. With Him was the most beautiful scent she had ever smelled. It was unlike anything she had smelled before. It was fresh, sweet, floral, clean, and colorful like the rainbow. His presence left a residue canceling out the hideous fog.

Jesus placed His right hand on the forehead of her earthly self, laying in time on the exam table. With His left hand, He placed it on her abdomen. At His will, not the doctors or her body, Jesus reached in, cradled the fetus, and then pulled it to his heart. A train whistle went off, and Jesus smiled because, in honor of Delaney's family legacy, this young one was having a birthday, and this would be its first day. He allowed Delaney to hear the whistle so that it would trigger the sweet memory with her family, but in an effort to disrupt, the enemy shot pain through her as a distraction. Immediately, Delaney's mind equated the pain with punishment and chose to believe it to be so. The revelation of what was actually happening in the room blew Delaney's mind. It was so different that the way she processed it!

A beautiful female angel appeared with Jesus, and she took the fetus and stepped back a few inches. Jesus leaned over Delaney's hysterical mind and body, stretching His arms out from end to end. Peace flowed out of Him and covered the table. Delaney settled down and noticed the clock saying 10:15 AM. She had always considered it the "Time of death," but Jesus looking up at the same clock, took note and declared it to the angels as the "Time of life." Delaney and Taven looking on from their eternal position could hear the celebration in the air and began to watch the most beautiful, delicate golden glitter fill the room. Jesus smiled and gently stroked the hair of time-stricken Delaney and whispered sweetly into her ear.

Delaney watches this all unfold and stands amazed that what was happening in front of her was going on as she lived it but didn't know it. It was all right there, but she didn't know. She expected Jesus to leave the room, but He turned to her and looked directly into her eyes. He reached up and brushed her hair aside as He had done to herself in time only seconds before. He gazed upon her, and she felt His actual person bloom from within her. He was inside her and before her at the same time. He had taken the sweet soul she thought she had killed and saved it.

Delaney fell to her knees and clung to His shins, but He broke her embrace, knelt down, and wrapped His whole being around her. He didn't need to say anything. His person was alive like an electric current, and He ushered into her body waves upon waves of love. He corrected every lie she had believed and restored her completely and totally in His embrace. She knew that her babies were safe and had been cared for by love Himself. It was odd, but she didn't ask Him to see them or if they were male, female, grown, or not. It simply didn't matter. He had loved and cared for them; but intuitively, she felt like she knew them already. Maybe she had always known them, and that is why she missed them so much over the years.

Jesus stepped back, and the angel stepped forward. She was beautiful with dark brown hair, blue eyes, and fine features. Her eyes drew Delaney in, and then came the realization that who she thought to be an angel was actually the aborted child all grown up. The eternal child had stepped into time to assist and bring healing to her mother. Because she had been present, she understood fully all that Delaney had gone through and the anguish and torment that would follow. She wanted to spare her the pain, but having stepped directly from the womb to Jesus, she felt privileged to walk with her family through time as a support rather than experiencing a world with so much pain. She had admired Delaney's courage to get back up and continuing living after the knockdowns. Many times, her daughter thought that she was the lucky one to have missed the worldly experience.

Delaney looked down to see if her daughter was still holding the aborted fetus, but she wasn't. She was holding Delaney's hand. Love flowed through them like a current. She also saw that her daughter was also holding someone else's hand. It was another female with dark blonde hair with bouncy curls. As Delaney looked into the woman's face, she was met with an exuberant, bright smile. The woman took Delaney's other hand, and the current flowed in a circle between the three of them.

Delaney knew she was looking into the face of her first pregnancy. It was Randy's sweet smile enhancing this beautiful woman's fine features. These aren't angels at all; they are her daughters, raised in heaven by Jesus, the Father, and Holy Spirit until Delaney could get here. Taven peers into the circle of love and wraps his arms around them all. It is evident that Taven and the girls are all friends. She didn't know how it could be possible, but she now felt "caught up" beyond the restraints of time in a relationship with them. It is as if she is fully realizing what has always been.

Bryce crashes into the circle, and everyone laughs. He always brings the fun! As they embrace, the room dissipates away, and they are in the beautiful flower-filled field by the barn. Bryce plops down into the spongey grass then they all follow. The smell is exactly what she had seen coming from Jesus. The flowers were the colors of the rainbow and vibrated with life while the aroma of their King visibly danced around them. She takes a deep, wonderful, appreciative breath. It was all worth it just to have this moment with them. There was no rush or place to be. She was fully known and also knew them fully. It was a wonder to experience it without any judgment, embarrassment, fear, or shame. There was no feeling of wasted time or regrets. They existed outside the constructs of time, and her spirit laid down into the feeling. Simply being with each other was the point of it all. She relished it with her whole heart. The One within her also delighted. This feeling, this experience, this existence was the very point of everything He had done.

CHAPTER 19

Abeautiful, wise-looking woman presented herself to Delaney with a kind smile that drew her in. Without even considering it, Delaney threw her arms around the woman as a warm welcome only given to a few trusted people, but here it seemed appropriate with everyone. Liquid love flowed between them, and it was energizing in a different kind of way. Her eyes spoke to Delaney's heart much like those of Jesus. Delaney knew that this woman knew her on a different level, and somehow Delaney knew as much about her.

After a few deep, peaceful breaths, the woman introduced herself, and her words were like salve to her soul. "My sweet girl. You have been my favorite for a very long time. I have followed your journey, and the King and I have had long discussions about you. You are from my lineage as I am your grandmother from seventy-seven generations before you. My journey left the station in 420 BC, where I grew up in Athens, Greece. The land was weary due to wars, famine, and plague. I never thought I would live a long life because most people I knew died from disease.

Our world was unpredictable, and our minds wanted some way to make sense of it all. We had many gods who controlled our circumstances. After my family died, I was given as a slave to work for an old man who later became famous, Hippocrates. It was the first time I heard someone say that sickness was not a blessing or punishment from the gods. He believed in environmental circumstances that caused disease separate from the wrath of a god or goddess. This thinking revolutionized my mind and relieved the cloud of fear and shame that I carried. I always wondered, *Who made the gods?* Could there be one God out there that made it all? It seemed reasonable to me. In my later years, another slave was brought into my owner's household. She was a Jewish woman. She introduced me to the one God, Jehovah. My life made sense after knowing He existed."

Delaney heard what this woman was saying to her, but she just couldn't get over the fact that she was her seventy-seventh grandmother! Delaney had to remind herself to focus and listen to what she was saying. The woman continued, "We had a very special bond before time was created. After being in Jesus' presence, I began to remember you. I followed your journey and supported you along the way. My experience of living through a plague and thinking we had done something to cause it played a big role in how I saw the world. I heard your prayers and saw the struggle you had losing your boys. You wanted to make sense of it just like I did and thinking you 'deserved it' was easier than not having an answer at all. I stepped into your life with God to minister to your wounds and soothed your mind. Your strength was remarkable, and it is an honor to know you and share a portion of your story."

Delaney was so confused. This is really taking her for a mental loop with thoughts running wild like, *We knew each other before the foundations of the earth? You came to me! You and God were there?* The connection with this woman was undeniable and full of joy. Because she didn't know what to say, Delaney just whispered, "Thank you." As she did, a flood of gratitude felt like it was pouring out of Delaney's chest into the woman's heart.

The grandmother asks Delaney, "Do you remember the birthday gift given to you by your mother and Kinsley on your fifteenth birthday?" Suddenly Delaney pictures her father's watch that she wore for the rest of her life. Grandmother responds, "We knew that you needed a connection back to your father because the pain of his death felt so strong that it could overtake you and distract you for caring for yourself and family. You kept pushing the pain further and further away. One day, I entered your journey in the present time and inspired your mother and sister to the idea of gifting one of his belongings to you. They chose the watch which I thought was a perfect and beautiful choice. In the supernatural, I could see the warmth of his love come over you that morning when you put it on. Dennis was so pleased and together we watched a small portal inside you open up to God's love. It was that tiny place that allowed you enough joy to keep going. It was the same place you accessed when the boys were born that made you an outstanding mother. There is a mighty river that flows through our line because you allowed joy to win. I am deeply and profoundly proud of you."

The grandmother continues, "One day, we will visit some special moments together." For now, you have someone who would like to take you on a quick adventure. She directed Delaney to look to her right and noticed Bryce walking toward her.

Delaney can never get enough of seeing Bryce. Her heart stretches and leaps at the sight of him. Delaney asks Bryce, "Are we heading somewhere now?" She can see why eternity is not boring. There is so much to discover, and the revelations are endless.

The woman interjects, "You are the grandmother to many even though you don't know it."

Delaney presents a puzzled look and thinks, *Is she speaking of my granddaughter, Jayden? But that's not many?*

Bryce answers, "The bonds our Father establishes cannot be broken. They are divine and as binding as blood. It's time for us to visit the future."

CHAPTER 20

A S WITH THE OTHER ENCOUNTERS, the floor turns to clouds then a beautiful kaleidoscope of light beams begins to dance around them. A train car comes into focus. From the outside, it appears to be shiny stainless-steel glistening with a halo of light. The car has rounded corners and a clear glass dome top and is connected to similar-looking cars. As they approach, Delaney notices a sense of anticipation like something monumental is happening.

Bryce leans into an open doorway and glances back at Delaney with a twinkle in his eye. He extends his hand, and Delaney gladly takes hold to step in. She is surprised to see an expansive, multi-level, futuristic laboratory within the train car. This wasn't at all what she expected. She thought to herself, *I'm going to have to get used to surprises.*

In addition to white-coated people bustling through the room, there are automated, futuristic robots equally as engaging as the humans and they all set about buzzing with purpose. The atmosphere is electric with anticipation. The beehive of activity seems to revolve around one woman. She is in her late thirties, tall, blonde, and beautiful. Bryce moves closer to her, so Delaney follows. The woman is orchestrating preparations for something. Delaney notices that her nametag reads "Amanda Wright—Director."

As Delaney contemplates who this woman could be, she notices a hush coming over the room as the door at the far end opens. An elderly, grey-haired man enters wearing a tweed blazer looking distinguished with glasses and a cane enters. Amanda raises her head to see the old man, and her whole face softens with love and adoration. As he walks toward her, every person settles quietly to watch what will happen next. As he moves closer, Delaney realizes that she too recognizes this man, but she can't quite place how. His tall, slim build is stately, and his fine features handsome. His eyes are mesmerizing, and she studies them for clues.

The woman opens her arms and says, "Dad, I'm so happy you are here."

The man replies, "I wouldn't miss it, pumpkin." With just that one sentence she recognizes his voice.

Delaney turns to Bryce and says, "Brady?"

Bryce nods in agreement that she figured it out. "Brady Wright, all grown up," Delaney commented to herself with tears welling up in her eyes. Bryce responded, "…and his daughter." They both turn to watch Brady embrace his daughter Amanda in the middle of this huge laboratory.

Delaney is so thankful to see Brady, one of Bryce's closest friends, and witness the love he has for his daughter. "Oh, Bryce, thank you for bringing me here," she said. Bryce nodded as a redirect for her to focus back on the two.

Amanda took a moment to gather the crowd and then introduced her father to the room, saying, "As many of you know, I became a researcher because of my father. He raised me to always preserver and never give up. His best childhood friend, Bryce, taught him many life lessons before leaving this world, and they were passed on to me as well as many others who knew him. 'Live like nothing ever happened' was a common saying in our household, and I am grateful to a man I never knew because it shaped the man I know as my 'Dad.'" Amanda continued, "My dad raised us to love other people and do what we could to use our gifts and blessings to honor God. It is because of this man that I began a journey fifteen years ago to identify the T-1 Cell Disorder and develop an antibody transfusion to eliminate the disease that affected Bryce and so many others. Today, my father, Brady Wright, has the honor of looking into this microscope as the first person to hopefully see the cure that will eradicate this disease." Amanda turned to her father and gently wiped away tears streaming down his cheeks. She said to him, "Daddy, when you are ready, please look into this microscope. We will know that the serum worked if you see dark red circles. If the circles are green, we will know that it did not work. Please give us a thumbs up or thumbs down, and we will turn on the screens."

Brady shook his head in agreement feeling a little unsure about being responsible for such an occasion, but Amanda had assured him that the result would be obvious. He was hoping with all his heart that he would see red because his daughter had dedicated her life to this moment. He embraced Amanda one more time and then leaned into the lens of the microscope. He adjusted his glasses slightly and looked in. After a brief pause, he raised back up and lifted two enthusiastic thumbs up into the air. The whole laboratory ignited in celebration. Several large screens came on around the room and what he had seen in the microscope was now visible to everyone.

The big red circles were indeed obvious, and Amanda stood completely still in awe of the scene in front of her. The man for whom she had never met would have been healed today. Inwardly, she said a prayer of thanksgiving to God for giving her the answers and she gave an internal nod to Bryce for being her inspiration. Bryce walked over and embraced Amanda and even though she could not see him, a smile came over Amanda's face as she felt a great sense of accomplishment and camaraderie with an unexplainable peace.

As the room celebrated, Amanda squeezed her left wrist and then raised it up for Brady to see. Brady gave her a nod of approval. Delaney couldn't believe her eyes. It was her father's watch! She had forgotten all about giving it to Brady when he visited her as a young man. He was newly married and expecting his first child. Brady had lost contact with she and Beckett with the busyness of life and stopped by to talk through some of his "adulting" challenges. For some reason, she felt compelled to gift him her most precious possession. Afterward, she wondered why she did it, but things had lost their meaning after losing the boys. She had shrugged it off. Now, she knew there was much more to her inclination to give the watch to her son's best friend. She began to think, "Bryce was probably there and led me to give it to him." She quickly shook her head as if to sort all the ideas zipping through her brain.

She looked at Bryce for confirmation of this new thought. Bryce picked up Delaney in a bear hug and twirled her around. He looked into her eyes and said, "Yes, I was there." Delaney felt another weight lift off her. She wondered how many amazing layers of misunderstanding could possibly come off. Bryce went on to say, "Mom, our lives do matter. Even from here, there is purpose in our existence before time, inside time, and outside of time. Nothing was stolen from us. It may seem like it when you are in the midst of time, but beyond that realm, there is purpose in all things because God makes it so. You are my precious mother, and you poured into all of us. Brady learned so much from us, and it became the fiber of his being. His daughter absorbed it, and hope was birthed in her through him. Jesus took something painful and made it a legacy of faith that will never be forgotten. It is one person's story, and there are so many more. You see, if you had asked me to die so that so many could live, I would have said yes. God would never have asked such a painful question to you and Dad, but your trust in Him allowed Him to make the best decision for the generations. This is our inheritance, and there is so much more. Your life is like the center of a pebble tossed into the stillness of time. You make ripples that endlessly travel on."

This was so much for Delaney to take in. Her head was swimming with uncatchable realities floating in her head. She always felt like a dark enemy cast a cloud over her as a little girl and somehow won every power struggle to cast doubt and rob her joy. So many times, she wondered if God was as powerful as she hoped, but it wasn't what she was experiencing. Much of her faith was built on the fear that if God wasn't loving, strong, and faithful, the realization of it would cast her into all-consuming darkness that would take away her hope of making it one more day. So, knowing she was so close to the edge of darkness, she chose to keep on believing. Delaney is seeing now that He truly is all that she believed and so much more. He is capable of weaving lives together brilliantly to accomplish a good plan, even during tragedy and sorrow. He can take any situation and redeem it for something better. She will forever stand in awe of His goodness.

As Delaney contemplates the complexities of God, she looks across the room and sees Jesus' sweet face looking back at her. He is smiling so big, and His eyes dance with color. She begins to notice among the present-time people; there are other eternals. Angelic beings, so bright and beautiful yet oddly familiar like friends from long ago. They are mixed into the crowd and share the same infectious smiles she saw on Jesus' beautiful face.

Jesus nods in her direction, and she is mesmerized by Him. Without moving any closer, she is able to talk with Him. Delaney thinks, "You did this, didn't you?"

Jesus laughs and replies, "I considered it all before I created the foundations of the world, even before time."

Delaney replied, "But each person and each situation? Each train car and its connections? How?" Her mind was spinning with the complexities of what she had just realized.

Jesus smiled and replied, "It's really My Father's doing. He is the one that dreams the biggest, and My Spirit is fully capable of executing whatever He desires. Together we delight in creation. Every tear was collected, every hope considered, and We enjoy expressing our love for you by working all things for your good. You thought I had turned my face from you, but there was never a moment that you were alone. I was with you in every struggle and made sure that only good would come from it all. You are only just beginning to understand how much I love you and take interest in every part of your life."

Delaney couldn't resist any longer and ran into Jesus' arms. His embrace felt big and soft like a cocoon hiding her from the rest of the world. She didn't have any more thoughts. Her spirit rested in His, and the beautiful silence lulled her to a new level of love and contentment. Nothing else mattered. Only her. Only Him. How wonderful He is! She wasn't even sure she was a separate being from Him. She felt so interconnected with Him that there was no beginning or end between her and Him. She didn't know how this could be, but she didn't care. Being one with Him is the only thing that matters. Delaney had never felt an embrace with no rush or inclination to stop. She could rest in His arms for all of eternity. She didn't think of needing to be somewhere or do something. She had no thoughts at all except the deep knowing that she was secure in His arms. Her beloved was hers, and she was His.

CHAPTER 21

D ELANEY WONDERED what would happen next. There would
be no way to top this experience, and surely there is nothing
left to do or learn here. She felt as though Jesus' presence had just
answered every question that had ever been in her heart. She was
content with Him and no longer felt the friction of unanswered
questions or expectations that were once the hard driver of her daily
existence. Here, she simply existed in complete joy and acceptance.
Her old self would never have believed it possible. Oh, how she
wished to revisit her twelve-year-old self to reset the dominoes so
that when they fell, the design of her life would be totally different.

Jesus sweetly asked her, "Would you really want to reset your
journey?" Just as quickly as she had the thought, His question now
made her wonder if she would. There was no pressure to answer, and
the point of the question was not to get an answer but to provoke
possibilities within many answers.

Jesus asked, "Would you like to meet Abba now?"

At one time, Delaney would have politely replied, "No, thank you,"
to this question because she was convinced the old, white-bearded
man on the judgment throne was anxious to strike her down and
avoiding Him for all eternity might be wise. But it surprised her when
her spirit leaped with excitement, and she immediately replied with
an enthusiastic "Yes, please." There was a surety inside her that Abba
Father was her true home.

The magnificent scene of the laboratory with the tremendous
celebration slowly faded away. They were transported through a
star-laden portal, granting Delaney the most incredible view of the

universe. Earth, her human home, was in the distance, and a beauti-ful array of light beams were shooting outward into the universe from the planet in an amazing array of colors. Some beams were bright and strong, and others were more subtle but just as beautiful. She mused, "I never saw these lights when I was there."

Jesus answered, saying, "The largest and brightest of lights are the prayers of mothers for their children. They are the most beautiful of all prayers. You had many of them, and I not only heard them, but recorded them, answered them, and cherished your heart for your children and others. I was most pleased when you gave it all to me, even your gut-wrenching cries filled with anger and bitterness. You let me see you down in the deep places." He paused remembering Delaney's prayers, then he turned his attention back towards the earth light beams and said, "Aren't they amazing?" Delaney's heart filled full with the love she sensed from Jesus for what was happening on Earth. She didn't understand how He could be so intimate with so many at once, but she was certain He personally knew of each beam of light, the cause, and the solution. He was in perfect control, and the whole universe would bow to His commands. Seeing this loving God with such strength be so relatable and intimate would always leave her in awe.

Their destination wasn't a cloud-filled chamber with thrones and angelic beings, but rather a beautiful, white sand beach with crystal clear water and a sky reflecting the colorful light beam prayers from the earth. As she looked around in amazement, Jesus seemed to take delight in her surprise. He knew the images of His Father she had in her mind were vastly different and Jesus took great pleasure in watching those stereotypes be broken into pieces. Delaney asked, "Are we here? Is this the place your Father lives? Here!" Delaney had envisioned a white-haired, old man dressed in a white toga sitting on a golden throne among a sea of white puffy clouds and angels playing harps.

Jesus chuckled and said, "Abba, we're here!" and looked towards a colorful hammock positioned between two beautiful palm trees. Delaney's attention was drawn to a set of toes peaking out on one end with an occasional wiggle. Then, a hand pulled down the beautiful, crocheted middle revealing a handsome, mature man with a contagious smile. His face was like Jesus but more defined with gentle wrinkles of wisdom.

Abba cheerfully greeted them with a voice that sounded like music and filled every part of her being. He invited Delaney to crawl into His hammock and sit a while with Him. Like everything else she was experiencing, she couldn't believe her eyes but was drawn in without any fear or hesitation. He opened it up for her to easily slide in.

As she snuggled up next to Abba, she noticed Him wearing a Hawaiian print shirt full of colorful flowers and little white butterflies. She wondered if those were "her" butterflies, and as soon as the thought entered her mind, He answered, "Why yes, they most certainly are yours,." As He said it, the delicate butterflies lifted off His shirt and began to fly around as if dancing to the melody of her heart. One landed on her hand and slowly opened and shut its translucent, silvery white wings so she could see them clearly. Each wing carried a loop of the infinity sign.

During her journey through time, Delaney had noticed a butterfly symbol on several of her train cars but didn't think to ask about it or even consider it to be significant. Now she knew it was no coincidence and marveled at how every detail matters to Abba. Abba interjected, "From long ago, I created this symbol especially for you. The infinity sign signifies life outside of time, or time trains as you have come to know it. The infinity sign rides on butterfly wings to honor the time your sons sent butterflies to encourage you to look beyond despair and refocus to hope. Even though it seemed like an impossible task, you allowed your eyes and heart to see past your pain and believe in love. I always knew it would be a beautiful moment worth commemorating. Together, Taven, Bryce, and I created this symbol and butterfly species especially for you. They are yours to take with you."

Delaney was puzzled at the last part, thinking, "Where am I going?" She had grown so accustomed to His presence that she didn't want to leave.

Abba continued, "Don't worry, child, you are home now, and all this I share with you. Whenever you want to talk, I will be here waiting for you. This is 'Our spot.'" She knew He wasn't speaking figuratively. It was a declaration that the Creator of the Universe, Abba Father, would be here, for her at any time, and they would share so many lovely talks and fun adventures ahead of them. He continued, "I'm glad you like our place. You were born with a love of the ocean and appreciation for an expansive, sky-filled view." Delaney remembered some of her most treasured memories at the beach included long walks in sand, catching fish off the pier, and naps to sound of waves rolling up on the shore. She was created by her Father to find great pleasure in the ocean as a way to connect and not lose sight of Him. So many times, she felt alone. But Abba was there, always drawing near to her, speaking through nature, people, and circumstance in a love language they shared. Delaney is grateful for the revelation of who Abba really is and how involved He has been in her life. Abba gives Delaney a slight squeeze and says, "There is another place that My Son prepared for you. I think you're really going to like it. We're anxious for you to see it."

Immediately, Beckett's sweet face looked over into the hammock and smiled. He loved seeing her at such peace wrapped up in the Father's arms. Delaney instinctively reached out and exclaimed, "Beckett! I've missed you!"

He effortlessly scooped her up into his arms and embraced her like never before. It was a long, sweet, reunion and full of complete understanding and acceptance. They were uninhibited by the shadow of their earthly insecurities and free to be one with each other. "I have something to show you," he said, motioning for her to walk with him down a path laid out before them. As they started to leave, she saw Abba and Jesus standing together, framed by the beautiful sea and colorful sky. They waved and then immediately engaged in a colorful, joyful discussion full of laughter, hand motions, and delight. Butterflies still danced around them, and the one that had rested on her arm was now perched on her shoulder. She always loved animals but never thought she would have a pet butterfly but was so glad she now did.

The path was nestled in among a combination of tropical trees and huge trees you would see in the mountains. The mixture of plants, birds, and flowers was amazing, and after a short time, the path opened into the beautiful wildflower pasture she had first seen upon arrival. The barn sat on the horizon, and she asked Beckett, "Is this our place?"

Beckett couldn't wait to show her everything he had discovered upon his arrival but knew they didn't need to rush. He replied, "Actually, the barn is a place Jesus created for me. It is so beautiful, Delaney. It is everything I ever wanted, and it is filled with treasures from our life together. I work in the barn and have so many projects to show you. The ideas I have here are so much bigger than anything I could have imagined. I sometimes collaborate with people that are straight out of the history books! Some may not have been famous, but led extraordinary lives and I am fascinated to work alongside them. One day you will have to come see it all."

As Beckett directed Delaney's attention over the hill behind the barn, he continued, "*This* is the place He prepared for you." The slight downward slope revealed a collection of farmhouses with a massive, landscaped courtyard full of blooming flowers. The homes were connected with walking paths and beautiful fruit trees. The homes were reminiscent of a Texas farmhouse but with so many additional details she had never seen before. It was as if many architectural styles had been incorporated into her ideal home to make it above and beyond what she could think or imagine. *Jesus really outdid Himself this time,* she thought. Beckett explained, "He knew that the one dream of your heart was to have your boys with you, happy and healthy. We are together, Delaney. All of us in one place! You will never fear a goodbye ever again."

As they step into the main house, she sees momentous from her life on earth, like the school pictures of the boys that once hung on her refrigerator are now framed on the most exquisite table, and she is greeted by her dog, Gucci. Bryce comes through the back door with his dog, Gidget. Her heart fills as she looks through a window to see Taven and Kirsten outside Taven's home, talking and laughing with Delaney's precious girls she has yet to fully discover. The thought of spending time with them is like an exploding goodness bomb going off inside her. This is so much more than she could have hoped for.

She turns to Beckett, and his smile washes over her with a knowing that felt so good. "So, we get to stay here together?" she asked.

Beckett replied, "Of course!"

Delaney said, "But I thought there was no marrying in heaven," half worried about his answer.

He replied, "I thought so too, but like so many things, we didn't have it all figured out when we were there. We just believed with the capacity we had and tried to make sense of it all, and not all scriptures were fully revealed to us at the time. I really think it was because we didn't ask or want to know anything different. I do know that our union mattered to God, and the depth of our journey has all cumulated into good. Jesus took it all and used every part of it for our good." He continued, "Your greatest desires and sorrows were not lost in Him. He really did prepare a place for you and for us from it all." Delaney took a deep breath of gratitude and decided to simply accept it all as an acknowledgement of how much Jesus loves her. She spent way too much time rejecting and scoffing at the love He tried to pour on her as a sacrifice for her shortcomings and mistakes. Now, she understands His love is a gift and her acceptance is an honor to Him.

Walking up from the garden is a tall, handsome man and having seen Brady not too long ago at the laboratory, she was reminded of him. She knew that it couldn't be him because they just saw him living in time. As he got closer, it was undeniable that it was indeed Brady Wright, here in her heavenly yard. She thought, *What the heck am I seeing?*

As with every interaction, Brady gave the sweetest, longest hugs to both Delaney and Beckett. Delaney asked Brady, "Did you die? When did you get here?" Brady chuckled and looked over at Bryce and Beckett. Together they all relished the idea of surprising Delaney with the most wonderful news. It created a symphony of excitement within Delaney that was almost too much for her to bear.

Brady replied, "I haven't died yet, Mamma D. I still have a few years to go. There will come a time when I breath my last breath on earth. Then, I step out of time and into eternity just as you have done. But on this side, there is no time. We are forever in God's presence and because of that we are forever in each other's presence."

Delaney thought for a good long while taking in all that she could from what he was saying. Instead of her thoughts speeding up, they were slowing down and settling into understanding. She mused, "So I have always been here?" She saw the three of them nodding slowing with anticipation for Delaney's understanding. "Why didn't I remember being here?" she asked.

Beckett answered her, "We all have old wounds from our time journey that need healing before we are able to move forward. You have revisited the lies that once caused you so much pain and God has applied His healing love. You are ready now to rest into eternity."

As soon as he said the word "rest," another layer came off of her making her feel as light as air. The feeling was incredible, and flashes of memories, people, and places begin to rush into her consciousness. Delaney remembers being present in eternity when Taven entered and watched him appreciate the legacy of love he had left behind. Next, she remembers seeing Bryce enter into eternity and together they witnessed the myriads upon myriads of prayers being sent up in his honor for many years to come by their friends, family, and sympathetic strangers. It's no wonder she feels like she knows people or has understanding that, at first glance, didn't make sense.

"We have history together!" she realizes. Knowing her daughters without spending time with them makes sense now because they have spent eternity together. With great excitement, Delaney screams, "There are no tears in heaven!" because she now understands there was no separation either in time or beyond. Oh, the majesty of it all! Delaney's appreciation for what God has created and how He made a way for an eternal existence will forever blow her mind. The evil one may have stolen lives from her at one point, but in reality and for eternity, he has no power over her and was rendered ineffective because they couldn't be separated.

As they watch Delaney "get it," Taven, Bryce, Brady, and Becket all release the most joyous laughter that fills heaven. All of creation reacts to it with sparkles, shimmer, and vibration.

The moment is monumental, and you are grateful and honored to have witnessed it. It reminds you of your own awakening and how the heavens celebrated.

CHAPTER 22

As you look over the beautiful homestead, you are convinced this is indeed Delaney's home. Every detail is handcrafted with her in mind. It is obvious that having her family around her makes her heavenly existence complete. It fills you up to the brim with happiness, having seen aspects of her journey that were once filled with despair, bitterness, sadness, and self-loathing. Now she is full of joy, understanding, love, contentment, and reward.

You know this is the end of your lesson, and you are grateful to Holy Spirit for guiding you through this intimate observation of a forever cherished, very dear soul. Delaney senses you are leaving and takes your hand and says, "Thank you for investing in my life and learning from my experiences. When first saw you on the day I entered over, I knew you had seen all of me too. It makes me feel good that someone else knows my story, the good and the bad. Being seen, heard, and fully known was once the greatest fear of my life, but it is now the security chain of freedom that undergirds me. I hope our shared journey helps you in some way."

You aren't sure how to answer Delaney. The transformed layers within you are so many it would be difficult to explain. The way she looks at you is so full of understanding. When Delaney was passing into the eternal realm, she looked at you with the same understanding and you wondered how it was possible. Now you realize there is an indescribable comfort inherent in meeting someone on this side.

You want to contemplate these things fully. It is all truly a miracle, the way the Creators designed it all and fit each life together in an individually unique, fulfilling way. You appreciate the realization that *relationships developing in heaven as they are on earth. Delaney's children didn't miss any time with her because once they left the time train, they stepped into a place that had no restrictions of time. They have always been together and will continue to be together. Within time, they each experienced their unique, purposeful existence; but eternity is the fullness of that experience. Delaney marvels at the scene outside her window and the men at her side, and you know Delaney's reward has been found here in her true, eternal home.*

Delaney turns towards you and asks, "Where did you start in my story?" You answer that it was all the way back to when the Creators were designing the world, specifically time. Several shades of vibrant pink sparkle dust begin to swirl around Delaney as her curiosity is ignited. Holy Spirit has a way of sharing a moment! The twinkle in her eye tells you an idea is coming. "Will you take me there?" Delaney asks. You can see the idea may have originated with Delaney, but now it has the glittery agreement of God on it. You happily agree and look forward to taking her to the grandest place in all of heaven, or at least that you have yet discovered. God has a way of outdoing Himself over and over!

Delaney's home fades away, and the beautiful train station replaces your surroundings. It is a marvel to see with its huge white pillars and massive windowed arches. Delaney is overcome by its grandeur and spins in a circle to take it all in, then spins again to take in more. The trains are all in their bays and quiet except for Abba, Jesus, and Holy Spirit's laughter. It rings out like the top melodic notes of an orchestra, and Abba's deep base laugh underscores it all. Delaney looks for them but can't see them, but you know where they are. You vividly remember the exquisitely carved table of old and where to find them. You take her hand and together set out to be with them.

As you round the corner, there they are, just as you remembered. Jesus is sitting back in a chair, giving a big belly laugh while Holy Spirit is dancing around the table, and Abba is standing with His hands on His hips, laughing hysterically. Delaney notices Abba has His Hawaiian shirt on, and there are a few white butterflies dancing in the air around Him. Her mouth is wide open with amazement, and you playfully reach over and close it for her. Now you are both joining in on the fun. Jesus motions for you both to come over and join them, so you do.

Jesus greets you, "Welcome! We're so glad to see you. What brings you by?" It was so casual and not how you once thought the triune God would be acting or talking. You giggle deep down at some things you once believed turned out not to be true at all and other beliefs were so much bigger! You know Delaney's mind must be spinning too.

You answer, "Delaney wanted to see where I started in her story. I told her at the beginning when you created time. She wanted to see it, so here we are."

Abba replied, "Well, that's a good place to start. I often come back to this spot Myself. Some of our greatest work has been spoken here."

Abba turned to Delaney and asked, "Where in time would you like to visit? Any place is possible from where we stand. We are outside time in the eternal place, but we can access it at any point along the way. The eternal ones are witness to all that happens within time, represented by these beautiful train cars that set out from this station to create what you once called 'history.' From this vantage point, we have access to all of it, past, present, and future, to observe and interact for the good of all.

"Where would you like to go?" Abba asked.

Delaney was a bit overwhelmed by the question because there was so much to see, but then Holy Spirit quietly embraced her, and with His presence, she simply knew what to say. She replied, "My life was defined by motherhood, and it is the greatest service of life both there and here. It brought me much pain but also great joy and healing. I would like to experience in part the life of the very first mother, Eve." Abba and Jesus exchanged a quick glance of pleasure at her answer. There was so much that Delaney would gain from knowing the first mother.

Jesus said, "Delaney, you were a mother among mothers, and knowing Eve and her story will bring you great joy and appreciation. I think it's an excellent idea."

One train, in particular, illuminates with excitement at knowing a new passenger will be boarding soon. As it catches your attention, the atmosphere begins to buzz with the excitement of what's to come. As Delaney walks towards the train, she too notices the colorful, vibrant coupler and chains between the cars. By its colors and how they respond as if living organisms, it is evident that these are no ordinary couplers and chains. They are the handiwork of the Holy Spirit whose job is to connect it all and keep it together. He moves through eternity with each and every one of us, holding it all together. At this thought, Holy Spirit dances around Delaney as He often does and leads the way onto the first step of a beautiful train car ornate with wood carvings much like the station. She notes a symbol very different than the infinity butterfly of her own cars and appreciates the creativity of her Makers and dedication to detail. She is anxious to learn its meaning.

It is time to leave your friend, who has also become a part of your own story. You embrace her and wish her well as she moves forward on a new adventure. Your surroundings slowly fade away, and your true, heavenly home comes into view. You always loved the mountains, and Jesus prepared the most beautiful valley ranch at the foot of the mountains specifically for you. Your guardian angel is outside on the front porch, pleased to see you have arrived. Beautiful voices can be heard from inside the log cabin singing to a musical instrument known only in this realm. It is the sound of love vibrating in the air, perfectly in tune with every cell of your spirit. The trees and wind join in and complete this welcome home symphony of laughter, chatter, and elation. It is so good to be home, and you realize the great honor is yours to share the overflow of all that you learned.

ABOUT THE AUTHOR

Thinking creatively has always characterized the way Susan Sledge approaches business and friendship. She enjoys weekends working with friends and family at the distillery she and her husband own together in their hometown in Granbury, Texas. They make hand-crafted spirits according to a family World War II recipe.

Susan had the honor of raising a son and daughter who are now grown and following their own dreams and callings. Her background includes a decade in environmental consulting in corporate America, starting three businesses, being the principal of a K-12 school, a decade working with business leadership students at Texas Christian University, and consulting for a non-profit.

She values the life journey with all its twists and turns, and discovering how seemingly unrelated experiences were, in hindsight, divinely designed.